Praise ɪoɪ
New York Times and USA Today Bestselling Author

Diane Capri

"Full of thrills and tension, but smart and human, too."
Lee Child, #1 New York Times Bestselling Author of
Jack Reacher Thrillers

"[A] welcome surprise....[W]orks from the first page to
'The End'."
Larry King

"Swift pacing and ongoing suspense are always
present...[L]ikable protagonist who uses her political
connections for a good cause...Readers should eagerly
anticipate the next [book]."
Top Pick, Romantic Times

"...offers tense legal drama with courtroom overtones,
twisty plot, and loads of Florida atmosphere.
Recommended."
Library Journal

"[A] fast-paced legal thriller...energetic prose...an
appealing heroine...clever and capable supporting
cast...[that will] keep readers waiting for the next
[book]."
Publishers Weekly

"Expertise shines on every page."
Margaret Maron, Edgar, Anthony, Agatha and Macavity
Award Winning MWA Past President

COLD
JUSTICE

by DIANE CAPRI

Published by: AugustBooks
http://www.AugustBooks.com

ISBN-13: 978-1-940768-31-1

Original cover design by Michelle Preast
Interior layout by Author E.M.S.

Published in the United States of America.

Visit the author's website:
http://www.DianeCapri.com

ALSO BY DIANE CAPRI

The Hunt for Justice Series
Due Justice
Twisted Justice
Secret Justice
Wasted Justice
Raw Justice
Mistaken Justice
Cold Justice
Fatal Distraction
Fatal Enemy

The Hunt for Jack Reacher Series:
Don't Know Jack
Jack in a Box
Jack and Kill
Get Back Jack
Jack in the Green

COLD JUSTICE

Thank you to some of the best readers in the world: Lisa Clayton (Marc Clayton), Justin Kemp, and B.C. Griffin (Jeannine Montgomery) for participating in our character naming giveaways which make this book a bit more personal and fun for all of us.

***And for Wilhelmina Boersma, trailblazer extraordinaire**.*

CAST OF PRIMARY CHARACTERS

Judge Wilhelmina Carson
George Carson

Justin Kemp
Marc Clayton

David Mason
Molly Mason
Leo Richards
Maureen Richards
Randy Trevor
Madeline Trevor

CHAPTER ONE

Traverse City, Michigan

THE DC-9 CIRCLED TRAVERSE City's regional airport, supplying a panoramic view of the Old Mission Peninsula and Grand Traverse Bay area that once had been our playground. Snow covered everything like a cozy comforter and I felt as if I'd been transported from my ordinary palm trees and sunshine world to a magical place.

George and I were a little too old, a little too sophisticated, to be so excited about a winter break. And yet, excited we were. This was our first vacation in years and I was as thrilled as a child who discovers her toys from Santa on a snowy Christmas morning.

We even left our dogs at home, which we almost never did. Harry and Bess, the lumbering Labradors who shared our life, would be fine, but we weren't sure we'd survive without them. We'd never been away from them before. Both of us had a little separation anxiety already.

Long, empty days stretched before us filled with anticipation and the promise of our favorite gifts. Hot chocolate, warm soups. Heavy sweaters, cozy comforters. Blazing fires in the fireplace. Good books. Good booze. Good cigars. No phones. No television.

Even better, no five-star restaurant for George to manage and no federal court justice for me to dispense. For an entire week. Our first real vacation in way too long.

The mere idea of a vacation had carried us through the last few days of hectic preparations and last-minute hearings.

And now, here we were, about to land.

Everything felt absolutely perfect.

Until things started to go wrong.

My self-induced amnesia began to clear. Memories surfaced, reminding me why I left this place a decade ago. For one thing, I remembered I hate the cold.

Unlike a down comforter, the snow blanket on the ground outside promised bone-numbing temps, sending shivers along my entire body. How could I have overlooked that? I wrapped my hands around my biceps and rubbed. Friction, I remembered, produces heat.

Ribbons of twinkling blacktop below nestled between high snowbanks plowed off to each side.

"At least the driving will be clear," George said as he peered across me to look out the window from his seat on the aisle.

He knew I hated treacherous driving in blizzards and black ice because a simple flat tire or fender bender carried the threat of chain reaction collisions and hypothermia.

George was a cold weather enthusiast, so all I said was, "True."

Blacktop roads were the only uncovered ground visible from the plane's window. Picturesque Traverse City nestled on the south side of the bay, which was recognizable only because I knew where the water *should* be. The Great Lakes had frozen to a depth of thirty inches this winter under all that snow, too. Record cold temperatures and snowfall combined to create the mountains of white gold that local ski resorts depended upon for revenue to support them through the lean summer months. Too much of a good thing, I thought, even as it all sparkled in the sharp winter sunlight.

A few minutes later, the captain delivered a perfect touchdown without sliding on the snow-packed runway and the entire cabin of passengers applauded. I'm not a nervous flyer, but the applause made me uneasy. Landing the plane smoothly was a big part of his job. Nobody applauded in my courtroom when I handled my cases especially well. But I imagined they might erupt in riotous celebration if I rarely managed the feat of handling my job.

Still, we'd arrived at our destination. Travel over. Our vacation officially began and I summoned as much of my prior excitement as I could muster.

We disembarked into the frosty jet way. Loaded down with parkas, boots, gloves and carry-ons, we hurried into the over-heated terminal. We made our way like pack animals to claim luggage and collect the rental.

How had I forgotten the sheer burden of moving around in a winter climate?

Half an hour later, with George behind the wheel of the rented Jeep Cherokee sporting a winter wonderland license plate and me trying to read the yellow highlighted route on the map because GPS was unreliable here, we traveled along the blacktop, skimming through the seven-foot snow tunnel open to the sky and the breathtaking beauty captured me once again.

Or maybe it was the frigid and unrelenting cold that stole my breath away.

Eventually, we reached U.S. 31 North, left Traverse City behind and headed toward Pleasant Harbor, about fifty miles north on the two-lane, according to the map.

We should have been there in about an hour. Ninety minutes tops.

CHAPTER TWO

THE ROAD HUGGED EAST Bay all the way up. The driving was easy. The day was gorgeous. *What's not to like?* I chided myself.

On our left was an unobstructed vista across frozen Grand Traverse Bay toward Old Mission Peninsula. Grape fields and cherry orchards barely poked above the snow. Shanties perched on the ice for fishing and there were a couple of ice boats, sails filled with blasting cold wind, racing back and forth. A recent storm had dipped even the smallest tree branches in ice gloves that sparkled in the sunlight.

We both wore our sunglasses, which seemed silly when the temperature here was exactly one hundred degrees lower than what we'd left at home this morning. According to the Jeep's thermometer, it was a frosty three degrees outside. Yet the sun's glare was brighter than back in Tampa.

Snow was piled five feet high on the right side of the road, exposing a view of nothing but a solid white wall outside the passenger window.

I reached over and flipped the fan to maximum and simultaneously pressed the button to lower the window.

George asked, more than a little testily, "I like the cold, but are you trying to freeze me to death?"

"Listening to the quiet," I told him.

The snow covered everything with a blanket of silence that muffled even the country sounds of the farmland we were driving through now. Except for what could have been snowmobiles in the distance, I didn't hear a cow or a horse or anything. Blissful silence.

"Well, can you just imagine the quiet?" George snapped. "I'm freezing my ass off over here."

I would have refused on principle alone, but it was really quite cold. I rolled the window back up, preparing to give him some lip about it, when we rounded a curve in the road and I glanced out the windshield.

"George! Stop!" I yelled and braced for impact.

He slammed on the brakes, both hands on the wheel. A sound like "Yaaaaaa!" exploded from his throat as he pumped the brake pedal.

Something oddly detached in my mind wondered whether pumping the brakes was the right thing to do.

The Jeep slewed into the oncoming traffic lane. George wrestled with the steering wheel and got back on track, but we continued to slide. Finally, the Jeep stopped.

Mere inches before we'd have slammed into the rear of the white Toyota SUV sitting dead still in the middle of our northbound traffic lane.

If we hadn't been wearing our seatbelts, we'd both have been thrown into the windshield. As it was, we were jerked back like snapped rubber bands. Fortunately, the airbags didn't deploy, although I wondered why not while my heart pounded like a thundering herd of wild buffalo in my chest and the sound amplified in my ears.

A few moments of silence enveloped the Jeep inside and out as we gathered our senses and discovered that we were not hurt.

The fluffy down parka I wore over a heavy wool sweater padded me enough that I might avoid a dandy seatbelt-shaped bruise across my torso tomorrow.

Otherwise, we were shook up, but fine.

"What the hell?" George eventually asked. His tone implied actual curiosity, a bit of his trademark composure returning. "There's not a sign of a taillight or a flasher on that vehicle."

The Toyota hadn't moved since I'd first glimpsed it. I could see no brake nor tail lights nor flashers of any kind, either.

And the engine was off.

If there had been snow on the road, the white Toyota would have been all but invisible. As it was, the blacktop beneath its wheels had provided enough contrast for me to see it. Thank God.

George flipped on the Jeep's flashers and unbuckled his seatbelt.

"Where are you going?" I asked him, still checking to be sure I hadn't broken any bones, trying to calm my heartbeat which was still pounding "Wipeout" in my head.

Without answering, he opened the door and stepped out onto the center of the road. "George?"

"I'll be right back. The driver may be in trouble here," he said, in what turned out to be the understatement of the century.

CHAPTER THREE

WE HADN'T SEEN ANOTHER vehicle for a while, and leaving the Jeep in the middle of the travel lane didn't seem wise. The snow wall on the right shoulder left us no choice. If another vehicle slammed into the Jeep, I didn't want to be sitting inside it. Time to get out while I still could.

After a couple of tries, I realized we were so close to the snow wall on the right that I couldn't open the passenger door wide enough to exit. *Swell.*

I wiggled around and lifted one long leg and ridiculously huge boot over the console in the middle of the Jeep's front seat, straddling the gearshift for a few moments before I managed to get the other leg over.

There are plenty of times when being almost six

feet tall is a real handicap. Climbing around inside of vehicles while dressed like a Laplander was one of them.

Eventually, I managed to get myself out through the driver's side door and joined George where he was standing, stock still, at the Toyota. His gaze focused straight ahead.

The first thing I noticed was the driver.

A man. Thirty-five, maybe forty. Impossible to guess his height or weight because of his position and attire. He was dressed in heavy winter gear like we were, except his hands were bare of gloves and very pink with cold.

His head was bowed and he slumped forward slightly, held in place by his seat belt. Maybe he'd had a heart attack or a stroke or something. Maybe he would be okay.

Why wasn't George trying to get into the car and help the guy?

My gaze rested on the Toyota's windows and I recognized the whole problem.

Involuntarily, my breath sucked in with a vacuum-like roar in the silence.

The driver's side window was shattered but still in place. The passenger side window was blown out, but a few shards remained, covered with blood and flesh and bone. And gray matter that could only have been the driver's brain. Some of the smaller grisly bits had already frosted over in icy crystals. The rest was probably embedded in the snow bank opposite where we stood.

My joy in this magic world had shattered, too, just like the glass on the Toyota's windows. Nerves hummed along my body unrelated to the frigid cold. Warnings I didn't heed.

The scene was surreal. A murder in the middle of nowhere, nobody around, the Toyota and its occupant blending with the pure sparkling snow but sticking out, too. Unmistakably murder.

The area felt sinister to me now, menacing. I looked around for the shooter, even as I knew he was probably long gone. If he were nearby, watching, he'd wear camouflage to make him invisible. Either way, I didn't see him. Which made things worse instead of better.

I'd seen gunshot wounds to the head that weren't fatal, but I could tell even from a distance that this wasn't one of them. Still, to be sure, I opened the door, pulled off my glove, reached through and touched his cold and bright pink flesh above his carotid artery to confirm.

He felt frozen, almost, which made me wonder

how long he'd been sitting here, dead or alive. The interior of the Toyota smelled like blood and frost. Or maybe my imagination conjured those odors because as cold as he was, the smells should have already dissipated.

I stepped back and re-gloved. The temperature was way too cold for unprotected flesh to be exposed very long without frostbite.

"Do you have your cell phone?" George asked me, his question grabbing my gaze from the evidence spatter.

In all our lives together, the more serious the situation, the calmer George got. It's one of the things that drives me crazy about him. Another man would have been shouting, panicked. In other words, normal. But not George.

"I do," I replied.

"Call the police," was all he said, as if the call would solve everything. Which, of course, it would not. No one knew better than me that discovering a murder victim led to years of pain for everyone involved.

But we couldn't simply leave the scene for someone else to discover, either.

So I pulled out my cell and made the call while I continued to scan for shooters.

CHAPTER FOUR

I MARCHED IN PLACE, trying to keep warm, which was impossible. Deep breaths drawn in through my nose burned all the way down into my lungs. Sunlight glared off the snow, blinding, even through my reflective sunglasses. Cold-induced tears seeped from the corners of my eyes and trailed warmth down my cheeks, lasting only a moment before all warmth evaporated with the saline.

George had crossed the two-lane road and was now examining snowmobile tracks on the side nearest the shoreline, opposite our two vehicles. No clue what he hoped to find over there, but I didn't feel like tromping around and didn't discourage his explorations beyond reminding him to be careful of the evidence.

We could have collected the victim and driven him back to town, but there seemed to be little point to that option, and it would have been counterproductive. Crime scene techs should sort this one out fairly quickly. As long as we could avoid a chain-reaction collision until help arrived.

The 911 operator had assured me that responders were on their way. The first to arrive would probably be from the Michigan State police post in Traverse City, she'd said. When I asked her how long it would take, she'd deflected. I looked at my watch. Only ten minutes had passed since the call and we were about an hour from town. I guessed we probably had fifty minutes of time to kill.

We remained alone with the body, the cold and the now-screaming quiet.

Seeking something useful to do that wouldn't destroy the crime scene, something mundane that would make the scene less real while it kept my circulation going, I looked in the back of the Jeep and found four small plastic orange cones and flares in the emergency kit.

I walked back from the Jeep to the curve in the road that blocked a traveler's view of both vehicles and put two cones in the northbound lane. Then, I walked the other two up to the southbound lane, about 100 feet in front of the Toyota. The cones might not have made us any safer, but I felt better doing something. Warmer, too.

When I returned to the Jeep, George had finished his survey of the snowmobile tracks and the rest of the accident scene.

"It looks like a rifle shot," he said, pointing to the shattered driver-side glass.

"Deer hunters live in this area and just about everyone knows how to shoot a shotgun," I replied. "But this looks like above-average marksmanship to me."

George was a handgun enthusiast. But I knew more about forensic evidence in firearm-related deaths than he did. Besides my personal experience at crime scenes, I'd also heard plenty of expert testimony on the subject.

"You think the killer shot at the car while it was moving?" he asked.

The possibility didn't seem likely to me. Any kind of drive-by shootings were fairly rare in Tampa, but out here they had to be non-existent. Even a highly-trained military sniper preferred not to aim at a random moving target, given a choice.

"Doubtful. Come on. Let me show you something," I replied.

George followed me up the road a little way and around the bend where I pointed to the snow covered pavement in front of the Toyota closer than the spot where I'd placed the orange cones.

"The wind has been gusting hard. Might have blown the snow over the road there," George said.

The road had been plowed clean. At some point yesterday or the day before the sun had heated the blacktop enough to melt any snow that had been left after the plow came through. We'd been lucky enough to drive on good road. Which was one of the reasons we hadn't slammed into the Toyota. The pavement was fairly dry and mostly clear.

Everywhere along the blacktop, that is, except the one spot.

"Look at this." George walked near the shoulder a little farther north. I followed him. He showed me where tracks indicated a snowmobile had left the snow and pulled onto the dry road, dragging some of the snow that had been on its runners along with it and transferring that snow onto the blacktop.

George said, "The snowmobile pulled up here and blocked the traveled lane of the highway." He gestured with his gloved hand.

"But the Toyota never got this far," I replied.

"So you think the snowmobile rider walked back and flagged the Toyota down?" George asked me, as if I had a crystal ball.

"That doesn't explain the broken driver-side window and the long-range rifle shot," I said. I stood where the snowmobile must have been parked and looked south toward the Toyota. "You can't see the vehicle from here because of the bend in the road and the amount of snow piled up and because it's white. If it had been a dark color, maybe it would have stood out."

I looked at George to see if he understood my meaning. He nodded, but I explained anyway, to be sure. "Not just a lucky shot by some guy taking target practice as the cars went by. The snowmobiler stopped the Toyota intentionally."

This was more bone chilling than the frigid cold air surrounding us, but I waited for him to recognize and verbalize the only possible conclusion. He got it fairly quickly.

CHAPTER FIVE

"WHICH MEANS THE SNOWMOBILER knew who was driving the car and wanted to kill him," he said slowly.

Hearing it from him didn't make the truth any better.

"It looks like a set up. Yes," I said.

I looked around again. Unlikely the guy would still be anywhere within fifty miles of us. But I didn't like standing out in the open like this.

George bent his knees and lowered his body so that his gaze was even with what must have been the snowmobiler's sightline. Then he stood and walked over to the snowmobile tracks on the other side of the road again.

"Let's not disturb the scene any more than we

have already," I told him, knowing only too well the number of problems a contaminated crime scene would present at the killer's eventual trial. And there would be a trial if I had anything to say about it.

Glancing at my watch again, I saw that only twenty minutes had passed since we'd first found the Toyota. I was thoroughly chilled outside by the weather and inside by the cold-blooded murder. Maybe the shock of the entire thing was starting to settle into my bones a little, too.

Without thinking, I took a deep breath and the cold seared all the way into my lungs again. A hint of pine scented the air and added to the burn.

George returned to the area where I'd found the snow on the road and looked at it more closely, squatting down to get a better angle. A stronger breeze had kicked up. Clouds of dry snow swirled fine white powder around us now, chafing my face and forcing my hands deeper into my pockets. One of my gloved hands connected with my phone.

Which reminded me that I should take some photos of the scene before the weather destroyed even more evidence. I removed my gloves to operate the camera and my fingers immediately stiffened as if my warm blood had immediately chilled to pudding.

The brittle cold had sucked humidity from the air and the snow. Snowmobile tracks on the road itself, if any had been there before we arrived, were blown away. By the time the state police arrived, the tracks would be completely gone, as if they'd never existed at all. No doubt the killer was counting on that very thing.

I grabbed as many snapshots as I could, blowing on my fingers from time to time to keep the joints flexible. Documenting the crime scene as well as possible under the circumstances.

George began to walk slowly back toward the Toyota until he reached it, then turned and walked forward again. I tagged along, partly documenting everything with the photos and a few minutes of video, and partly to keep warm. It wasn't until we were at the bend in the road ahead that he stopped again.

"What's bothering you?" I asked.

"From here, I can see the Toyota. But I wouldn't have been able to put that shot through the side window. The angle's wrong," he told me. George has won several marksmanship prizes over the years. If he couldn't have made the shot, it probably couldn't be done. At least, not by a recreational deer hunter.

The implication in his words coiled my stomach into knots. I pulled the parka's hood over my head, re-gloved and stuffed my hands deep into my pockets to warm up. And to stop the shaking.

I looked around. The crispness now present in the air further sharpened my awareness. "The snowmobile driver had an accomplice. Two people who wanted this guy dead instead of only one."

We remained easy targets, standing out here, I thought again as I looked around once more, but saw nothing unusual that I hadn't noted before.

"Maybe." George continued walking toward the car, looking around on the ground. A fine powder of white snow now dusted wide swaths of the road, while in other spots, the black asphalt was clear. No particular pattern revealed itself. The wind whipped the snow now in gusts that stayed only moments and then blew away.

George was looking down, walking slowly, one foot in front of the other. I walked behind him, looking backward, still concerned that another car might come along and slam into us, or the shooter might lay in wait, or a thousand other things could happen.

You never see the bullet that gets you.

We saw no one. The wide red line on the map suggested this was a busy road, but we had not seen another car for almost thirty minutes. Maybe the shooter had known the area well. Maybe he'd known the roadway would be deserted. Made sense as a working hypothesis, at least.

My teeth had started to chatter and my nose was running, too. Dying from exposure wasn't what I'd had planned for our vacation. And I was feeling so cold now that I began to wonder how long it would take me, a thirty-nine-year-old woman, five feet eleven inches tall, warmly dressed, to succumb.

But then I saw something I'd missed.

"Willa, let's wait in the Jeep. I'm freezing," George said, before he began walking in that direction. He'd apparently satisfied his curiosity. For now.

I barely heard him.

About five feet in front of the Toyota, I bent down and stared at the ground.

"What is it?" George asked, a little irritably, when he walked over to join me.

I pointed with a gloved hand to a couple of marks in the snow, very faint. "Doesn't that look like something heavy was placed there and then removed?"

He looked at the snow where I'd pointed. "Maybe. Like what?" George looked back at the Toyota. Almost immediately, he saw what I'd seen.

The Toyota's right front tire was flat.

"Maybe a board or something with a sharp spike in it. It's hard to say. But it worked effectively to stop the Toyota," I replied.

We hadn't noticed the flat tire before because we'd been walking along the left side, away from the snow wall on the right shoulder of the road.

It took George a few long seconds to realize what the flat tire meant. When he figured it out without any further comment from me, the knots in my stomach pulled tighter and I began to shiver so much that when George stood up and turned to face me, he actually noticed.

"Here. You're freezing," he said, wrapping me in a big hug for body warmth.

Before we could say anything more, the promised Michigan State Police trooper pulled to a stop behind the Jeep.

I don't think I'd ever been so glad to see a cop in my life.

CHAPTER SIX

EXACTLY FIFTY-TWO MINUTES after we had
called, the state trooper arrived in an old-fashioned
navy-blue patrol car with a single red flashing
gumball on the top. Must have stopped for donuts.

Thank God the driver of the car was beyond
help when we'd made the call or he'd have died
waiting.

The trooper approached and we introduced
ourselves. "I'm Trooper Justin Kemp," he said,
handing George a business card. It was hard to see
what he looked like in the blinding sunlight,
through my sunglasses, while he wore that big
brimmed hat and sunglasses. He seemed friendly
enough, though.

I pulled out my cell and snapped a couple of

pictures of the flat tire while George told Kemp what happened and what we'd concluded from our preliminary investigation.

"Mrs. Carson, Mr. Carson," Trooper Kemp said as he tipped his old-fashioned hat with the flat, wide brim that shadowed his features more than it should have. "Please don't take this the wrong way. I mean you no disrespect. But we will conduct our own investigation and analyze our own evidence and come to the conclusions the evidence supports."

His attitude got my back up, so I said, "There's no question about it. There were at least two people involved. And it was a set up. For sure. While we're standing here, the killers are either getting away or taking aim. Which do you think it is?"

He replied, "There's a blizzard on the way according to the weather reports. The forecast says we'll be walloped with four to five feet of drifting snow before this one passes through. Teams are on the way here now and we need to get this crime scene cleared while we still can."

George and I had dealt with police officers many times before. They generally felt they were better at doing their jobs than we were. Sometimes, they were right.

Sometimes, not so much.

Today, I was more than glad to leave the young trooper to his work. He was right that the evidence had already begun to deteriorate and a blizzard would make processing the scene impossible. I was cold, and tired, and I didn't want to stand around out here and argue. I wanted a warm bath and a stiff drink.

Not necessarily in that order.

When we didn't protest, Trooper Kemp said, "I do need to take a tape-recorded statement from you and then I'll let you go on your way."

"We'll do the recorded statement later, when you're finished here. We have some questions for you, too." I reached into my pocket and pulled out one of my official business cards with the raised gold seal issued by the United States government to all Federal District Court judges. "My cell phone number is on the back. We'll be staying with Marc Clayton, in Pleasant Harbor. You know him, don't you?"

"It's a small community, ma'am. Everybody knows everybody here."

He took my card and glanced down to read it and the hat brim completely covered his face. When he looked up, he raised his hand to tip the brim again, slightly more respect in his tone this time when he said, "I'll stop by this afternoon if weather permits, Judge Carson."

"Or we'll call you," I promised.

I hooked my arm through George's and led him toward the Jeep. The trooper walked with us as if he planned to make sure we went on our way. While I struggled to maneuver myself over the console and into the passenger seat again, George asked, "So you knew the victim, then?"

Trooper Kemp seemed to be about the same age as the man in the car, maybe thirty-five, maybe a year or five either side. If they were both local, they'd have known each other. He probably shouldn't have answered, but he must have realized a judge could be trusted and we could hang around all day if he didn't.

Kemp said, "His name is Leo Richards. He owns the hardware store in Pleasant Harbor. He's married to Maureen and he has a little girl." As George moved toward his seat, Kemp added unnecessarily, "I'd appreciate it if you wouldn't say anything about this until we get a chance to notify the family."

"We don't envy you that job," George told him as he settled into the driver's seat. He turned the ignition on and the heater to full blast. Maybe the car would warm up again so that we could both thaw out someday.

We snugged our seat belts a little bit tighter this time and George carefully pulled out and around the Toyota. My desire to take pictures of the snow had evaporated, which was good because the phone's battery was low and I didn't want to run it out completely in case we needed to make another call. The phone charger was packed in one of the suitcases. I could charge up once we reached the cottage.

As we drove north, away from the scene, I glanced into the side mirror. Kemp stood, holding a cell phone to his ear, watching us go, maybe calling in our license plate or something. Two vehicles with flashing lights pulled up behind him. Probably part of his team. When we rounded the first curve, I lost sight of Kemp, but I still wondered who he'd been talking to.

There was no rush to take my statement. I wouldn't forget anything about the man with the pink hands and the hole in his head and his brains splashed all over the inside of his frosty vehicle. No chance of that. No chance I'd let this murder remain unsolved, either. It might not be my jurisdiction, but justice is always my job and I liked it that way. Judges are like cops. We're never off duty.

"You sure know how to start a vacation," I said, once my teeth stopped chattering, already thinking about the next steps.

CHAPTER SEVEN

WE CONTINUED ON OUR way toward Pleasant Harbor in silence. The clean snow had lost its appeal and clouds had moved in to replace the sparkling sunlight just as our vacation's luster had dulled. We traveled with our separate thoughts for companionship, until a small sign on the right hand side of the road caught my attention.

"Welcome to Pleasant Harbor. Population 1,202," I read aloud simply to break the silence. *Now only 1,201.*

The first flakes of the promised blizzard began to fall. George flipped the windshield wipers on and stopped at the traffic light.

Smoke rose from the buildings to our left where U.S. 31 abutted Michigan Highway M-244. Once again, the area seemed deserted. In the summer, a line of traffic stopped here and then filed off in all directions. Not today. The hardy residents were probably huddled inside by their fireplaces, which was where I'd hoped to be by now.

Many times we'd turned right at this intersection to continue on toward Mackinaw City and then to romantic getaways on Mackinac Island. But today, we'd turn left to downtown Pleasant Harbor.

The light turned green and we travelled a bit farther into town before George said, "Looks pretty much the same as the last time we were here, don't you think?"

"It's hard to tell with the snow covering everything, but I don't see very many new buildings, if that's what you mean." I wanted conversation, but discussing the town or the weather seemed so banal now. I didn't feel like socializing. My thoughts continued to return to the murder as if a video loop replayed in my head. There was something else about it that was odd, but what was it?

"What if we take a short ride through town and head to Eagle Creek Cafe? It's late, but we might still get lunch." I didn't say anything. "Or we could go directly to the cottage now, if you'd rather get unpacked." More silence. "Willa?" He took his right hand off the steering wheel, where it had been firmly planted since we'd returned to the Jeep, and placed it over mine in my lap. His gloved fingers intertwined with mine.

I said, "I've seen murder victims before. I just didn't expect to find a gruesome one this afternoon."

"I know."

"The landscape looked soothing, so pristine and beautiful."

"I know."

"A man murdered in a tiny, peaceful hamlet shakes your faith." That was my problem. I kept forgetting that the gun lobby is right about some things. It is people who kill people. Environment didn't change basic human nature.

"Confining humans in a small space as harsh as this one and expecting them to peacefully coexist is probably too much to ask for." George squeezed my fingers a little tighter to signal that he needed his hand back. I let him go and felt immediately bereft.

Snow was falling faster now. He increased the wiper speed.

Something more about the crime scene still

niggled at the back of my brain. But it disappeared around the corners whenever I almost grasped it. The best thing was to treat it like a timid kitten and wait until it came far enough into the open to seize it.

George had turned the Jeep onto Main Street. "Let's get some lunch. We can meet up with Marc and maybe find something else to talk about for a while," he said.

"You just want to get to Marc and talk shop, don't you? Have you forgotten you're on vacation?"

He laughed and said, "Have you forgotten you're on vacation, too?"

"Fair point." After that, I sat with my thoughts.

We traveled over the drawbridge on the west end of Main Street, which was perpetually down in the winter since the river froze and no boats could pass through anyway. The snow had been plowed from the grates of the bridge and the Jeep's tires chirruped as we passed over.

George turned right and traveled along the winding street that followed the shoreline, the frozen edge of Lake Michigan stilled now in ice hard enough to drive snowmobiles across. On the left side of the street sat stately nineteenth-century mansions from a bygone era when the town was ruled by lumber barons.

Nothing much seemed different, though.

Back when George and I were Detroit residents, we visited Pleasant Harbor often. It was a lovely resort town, summer and winter, back then. The deep, cold lake was beautiful in a way completely different from the Gulf of Mexico that surrounds our home in Tampa. Golf resorts and ski resorts and wineries and outdoor activities abounded nearby. Although the population triples with tourists who bring along their Grosse Pointe and Birmingham and Chicago suburban money as well as their big city values, I'd never felt threatened or vulnerable to violence here.

Had the town changed that much since we'd moved south?

True, only those sturdy souls who can survive over 200 inches of snow and subzero temperatures with high levels of humidity, exist here full time. Theirs wasn't a lifestyle for the faint of heart. Meaning it wasn't a place where George and I chose to survive. We'd known that back when we lived here and we knew it now.

I considered what George had said about the harsh winter conditions these folks lived in. Maybe, if you were forced to stay here year round, it was like a prison. A beautiful frozen prison, sure. But still a prison. Perhaps cabin fever set in too easily and led to depraved inmate behavior. Seems I read something about cannibals in Wisconsin once.

Which wasn't an excuse for murder. Never had been. Never would be. We prosecute those who kill in prison, too.

The curious thing was how pink Richards' body was. I'd seen it before in autopsy photographs of carbon monoxide victims. But this guy hadn't died from any kind of poisoning, obviously.

The more I concentrated, the less I understood, so I let it go. Temporarily.

CHAPTER EIGHT

WE CROSSED OVER INTO what had once been no-man's land and was now, perhaps, some of the most desirable real estate in Pleasant Harbor.

Milliken Boulevard was a picturesque four-lane that had once divided the town in half, separating the regular citizens on the east side from those confined in the asylum on the west side. A train ran between them alongside the boulevard for good measure.

"Would you have lived there?" George asked, pointing toward the castle-like estate ahead.

The former Eagle Creek State Hospital had once been another type of prison. A jewel in the crown of medicine so bright it had boasted a two-year waiting list for new patients. I believed the waiting list had resulted back then partly because conditions in the asylum were better in many ways.

"I'd have tried," I said, only too happy to embrace the distracting change of subject.

"Why?"

"The hospital was fully equipped with electricity long before the town. That alone would have enticed me to enter."

"Because?"

I was a constant reader and he always teased me about it. "Light to read by at night instead of an oil lamp or a candle."

He laughed. "But surely that's not all?"

"Two more things."

"Which are?"

"Remember I took that tour of the place when we were here last time? Did you know it had two sets of underground tunnels, one for its sophisticated steam heating system and another for moving people that connected the buildings? Thus," I raised my index finger, "heat without hassle. I wouldn't have had to chop wood or haul coal. And," I raised my second finger, "asylum residents never needed to venture outside in the damn frozen tundra. That sounds like heaven right about now."

We'd entered the grounds. Various buildings

were spread over several acres of what was probably lawn under all that snow.

"This place is amazing and beautiful and awful and creepy all at the same time, isn't it?" George asked.

It was.

Through sixty years of its history, the grand old buildings served as an asylum for patients with communicable diseases, mental disorders and, it was said, a place to imprison uncontrollable menopausal women.

As treatments and vaccines and pharmacology improved, budgets dwindled until the facility eventually closed. That was long before we moved to Tampa. Over the decades, some of the buildings had been condemned and demolished. Restoration of the others had to have been a nightmare.

"What happened to the patients, I wonder?" George asked.

"Our tour guide said there weren't many left at the end. The last few were simply released. They literally opened the doors and let them walk away. Which increased the local homeless population exponentially," I replied.

Could one of them have murdered Leo Richards? I quickly shook my head as soon as the idea surfaced. The murder was too well planned and executed to have been the work of a mental patient.

These days, the entire Eagle Creek Village complex had been reborn into a multi-use historical district filled with specialty boutiques, offices, condominiums, apartments, an inn, and restaurants. Some things hadn't changed much, though. Eagle Creek Village also boasted a two-year waiting list as its predecessor had.

"They're doing a masterful job with the restoration," he said.

George turned left down a two-lane driveway that opened onto a flat gravel lot. He parked the Jeep near the front door of what had once been the sprawling main building of the hospital and was now called Eagle Creek Village Center. This was where our friend Marc had relocated his Cafe.

There was no sign out front. For many years the only five-star restaurant in Northern Michigan, Marc's tony eatery didn't need a sign to advertise its presence to potential diners. Word of mouth had kept the restaurant full to overflowing when it had been located a few miles south of town. Now that it was housed in prestige and surrounded by history, reservations stacked up like magic.

George turned off the Jeep and looked toward

me. "Let's not talk about the murder to Marc. I'm sure he'll find out soon enough."

"Works for me."

Trooper Kemp would be calling this afternoon. More statements would be required after that, maybe testimony at some point. The process would be endless, even if the locals were up to the challenge of apprehending the killer. If that didn't happen quickly, then I'd become more involved than I already was. A quiet hour or two before the next episode seemed like a great idea.

George took my hand and squeezed it. "Come on, Mighty Mouse. I'll buy you lunch. Fortify you for crime fighting later."

He jumped out before I could hit him with a snappy comeback.

CHAPTER NINE

GEORGE CAME AROUND TO open my door and I left the warmth of the Jeep's interior for the unrelenting cold. Snow was falling heavily.

Under the snow, Eagle Creek's grounds were beautifully landscaped with wild English gardens. The lawns were dotted with tables and chairs under tents around a large lily-pond for alfresco dining. One of the old buildings had been demolished and its foundation converted into a bocce court. George and I had spent many idyllic evenings engaged in just such pursuits.

None of that was visible now.

It was March second. In three weeks, the calendar would declare spring. In Pleasant Harbor, Mother Nature would ignore the declaration for at least eight weeks. I remembered one Fourth of July when the temperature only reached forty-four degrees and the crazy ones in our group had insisted on swimming anyway. The memory alone made my teeth chatter.

The parking lot had been plowed to pack down the snow, but bits of gravel showed through here and there. Snow piles higher than my head outlined the edges of the lot. Several other vehicles, including a few snowmobiles, were parked and snow dusted, suggesting they'd been there a while. The entire grounds, except the entryway to the main building, were covered by even more snow.

"Let's get inside," George said, as he pulled his parka hood to cover his head and took my arm. I raised my hood and followed along, head down. We slid along the length of the plowed sidewalk, trudged up the stairs to the front door and stepped into a warm and inviting piece of history.

We waited at the hostess stand because the Cafe's main dining room was busier than we'd expected. Restaurants are usually quiet at three o'clock in the afternoon and the chef is busy with preparations for dinner. But Eagle Creek Cafe buzzed with conversation.

A couple of minutes later, the hostess returned to seat us. "Are you folks joining the bridge club? Mrs. Trevor didn't tell me she expected more members. You're a bit late and we've already closed the buffet, but we can find you a table in the back if that's okay and we'd be happy to serve you something from the menu."

"We're not with the club. Simply here for one of your amazing meals, please," George replied.

She collected the menus and, a little relieved, said, "Certainly. Right this way."

We were led to a table close to the kitchen and near an exit door, past several full tables of bridge players and a couple of lingering groups who seemed to be finished but reluctant to leave the warmth inside for the blizzard outdoors. Or maybe they weren't aware of the blizzard because the Cafe was located in what had once been the basement of the building. The windows were small and square and high on the walls. Seated diners would have to look above their heads to notice the storm and they were more focused on their meals and bridge games.

"I'm sorry that this is our last table. But the bridge club has filled the restaurant to capacity. Usually they're gone by now, but Mrs. Richards said it was tournament day or something like that," she said.

Mrs. Richards? The name hit me like a quick Taser hit.

George, ever the gallant restaurateur, replied, "This will be fine. The food will be marvelous no matter where we're served, I'm sure."

"Thank you for understanding," she said, leaving our menus and dashing off to a table of four women, three of whom looked enough alike to be sisters, and a fourth who seemed to be annoyed at their lack of concentration.

George grinned. "The dreaded Mrs. Trevor calls, I presume."

"Maybe," I said, quietly. "But is Mrs. Richards the victim's wife?"

"In a town this small, she's got to be a relative, at least."

Once upon a time, the cafe's kitchen was the site of the hospital morgue. Not an appetizing factoid right at the moment, to be sure, so I didn't mention it to George. Instead, we talked about this and that, avoiding the subject of our grisly discovery until after our food was presented.

One thing about a gourmet restaurant, it's usually stocked with fabulous ingredients for all sorts of wonderful food. Even if a guest arrives in the middle of the afternoon, on a weekday, in the middle of a blizzard, they won't go hungry.

We ordered Gouda cheese omelets with fresh chives, toast with butter and locally made tart cherry jam, and a stainless carafe filled with nectar of the gods. Until the coffee aroma wafted to my nose, I hadn't realized I was so hungry.

George fell in like a man who hadn't eaten in a year. I picked up my pace.

The conversation noise level in the room and our isolation near the kitchen and the exit presented an opportunity for a private discussion. There was only one subject on my mind.

"Premeditated murder, obviously," I said. I willed him to test my conclusions aloud, hoping I'd made an error or missed something important.

He nodded between mouthfuls.

"I'm thinking the right handgun from the proper distance would produce those results," I said. "It looked like a rifle shot, but sometimes it's hard to tell for sure before the forensics are completed."

These had to be the best eggs ever. I actually hate eggs, so maybe they tasted great because I hadn't eaten anything at all today and my stomach had been tied in knots since I'd first seen the

Toyota. The cheese probably had something to do with it, too.

I finished my thought process to get us on the same wavelength. "The killer put something in the road to stop the car with a flat tire. He's close to the car and the victim. He wouldn't have remounted the snowmobile, returned to the field, aimed and fired a rifle to cause the effects we saw at the scene. That would take time and be a huge hassle and someone could easily have come along to witness everything. None of that is reasonable. A handgun is a better answer."

"Makes sense," he said. He warmed up his coffee from the carafe and poured more for me. "Unless the victim was the unlucky lotto winner of a random shooting."

"Then why not just shoot as the vehicles passed by and hope to get lucky instead of setting up a flat tire to stop one?"

"And the accomplice?" he asked.

"There to help make the job go faster, probably. Or maybe they were worried the driver would put up a fight and they'd need two people to subdue him. We won't know what their thinking was unless we find them and they tell us," I said.

"So someone who knew the victim knew he

would be traveling that road this morning. The killers laid in wait to execute him," George said. "Is that about it?"

This was the only reasonable conclusion and I'd reached it an hour ago. But I'd wanted another answer and after a while, I'd found one.

George piled tart cherry jam on the toast before taking another bite.

"Actually, I think it's worse than that," I said.

There certainly were worse ways to die than being shot in the head. I had presided over countless criminal trials and accepted dozens of guilty pleas. Killers admitted variously depraved murders for both logical and insane reasons. I refused to organize killers into classes, some better and some worse. Killing another human being was crossing a Rubicon to me. Justice for that should always be swift and sure.

It was the intellectual aspect of the murder that had captured George's imagination, though. He was a good strategist. One of the best. He enjoyed figuring out both the good and bad puzzles in life. So I waited to see if his conclusion was the same as mine.

Finally, he said it. "The killer arranged for the victim to be in that place at that time."

My breath snagged. I'd wanted to be wrong. An orchestrated execution with a high level of premeditation. A smart killer, a planner. Someone who deliberately intended to end a human life and get away with murder. Someone who knew how to make that happen.

If killers were classified by degree of guilt, and that is how our legal system operates, then the cold-blooded executioner was the most heinous.

What could a Pleasant Harbor hardware store owner with a wife and young daughter have done to inspire such malice? Sometimes, the depravity of my fellow humans made me want to hide in a hole like a groundhog, never to come out, even to predict the spring.

George continued talking almost to himself now, trying to work it out. "Predictability was required. What makes the most sense to me is the killer called Richards on a cell phone and told him something that caused him to travel that road at just the right time."

The eggs didn't seem so tasty any more, and I pushed my plate away. "But the victim lived here. His car was traveling *toward* Pleasant Harbor, not away from it. How do you explain that?"

"I can't explain it, except to say that the killer

must have known Richards' plans for the day or somehow participated in them." George finished his coffee, ate the rest of his toast and jam. The conversation didn't seem to be affecting his appetite at all.

My coffee was cold and the omelet congealed, half eaten and unappetizing now.

Eventually, he pushed his empty plate aside. "You may not get more food for a while," George told me in the same way a mother might scold a child.

"I guess I'll have to take my chances," I replied.

George refilled his coffee, offered me a fresh cup. I shook my head and pulled my parka over my shoulders. "We probably saw him out there. You realize that, right?"

We'd seen snowmobilers skimming along the edge of the lake on the way into town north of the crime scene. At the time, I'd thought the riders were lucky to be enjoying fresh trails. After we found the Toyota's flat tire, a more sinister image intruded.

As if conjured by our conversation, I heard the unmistakable sound of a snowmobile pulling up out front. At first, I thought I was imagining it, but when the engine died, profound silence reinforced the prior noise.

I looked toward the exit door. Stomping on the porch, probably the rider knocking snow off his boots. The level of tension in my body had escalated to the point where I almost jumped up to hide. As ridiculous as it seemed, it somehow felt possible that a killer was about to enter the room.

George made no move to rise, but he must have sensed something. As he had back when we were in the car, he reached over and placed his hand on top of mine. This time, the gesture didn't reassure.

CHAPTER TEN

THE BACK DOOR OPENED and an Eskimo powered through. A huge man, maybe three hundred pounds, wrapped from head to toe in navy blue down-filled Gortex. His face was covered by a black ski mask that revealed only his eyes, nose and mouth. Steam radiated off him. Oversized boots and gloves made his feet and hands look the size of tennis rackets. He stomped his boots to knock the last of the snow off onto the mat.

When he pushed the fur-trimmed hood of his parka away from his head and yanked off the ski-mask, his face looked reddened by the cold. White skin with a few freckles. Brown hair, brown eyes, bushy brows. Totally ordinary. Which didn't mean he was innocent.

Witness after witness who testified in my courtroom describing a killer usually said, "He looked so normal." Or, "He was such a nice man."

Sure he was nice and normal, until he deliberately caused a blowout of one of your tires and then executed you with a single bullet to the head.

Could this guy have been today's shooter?

"Hello, folks!" he said to us, in a rather jovial way for a cold-blooded killer. "I see the bridge club is still at it. Those women have some stamina, don't they?"

He huffed and puffed with the effort of removing his snowmobile suit over the girth of his stomach. As he hung each piece of gear in a closet by the door, he kept talking. "I'm David Mason, one of the chefs here. I ran out of butter, if you can believe that."

He held up a grocery bag heavy with several pounds of something inside. Square boxes were evident inside the thin plastic bag once he'd finished uncovering himself and moved toward us. Ordinary butter in a normal grocery bag. That's all.

"Hope you're enjoying the food," he said.

"We are, very much," George replied and he stood and shook David's hand and introduced us. "Is Marc with you?"

"Marc had a family problem to take care of."

"Nothing serious, I hope," George said.

"I'm not sure. He asked me to make you comfortable and say he'd meet you at the cottage," he glanced up at one of the high windows. I followed his gaze. "You might want to get going soon. Weather's a mess out there. In fact, I see the president of the bridge club over there sitting with my wife. She should be heading home, too."

"He's right, George," I said, rising from the table and gathering my gear.

"Let me walk you out," David said.

On the way to the exit, we stopped at one of the tables where four women were playing bridge. David laid a hand on one woman's shoulder. "George and Willa Carson, this is my wife, Molly. And her sisters, Maureen Richards and Madeline Trevor, and our good friend Jeannine Montgomery."

Madeline Trevor gave me a strange look I couldn't decipher, but the others were friendly enough. We smiled and nodded all around before David explained the blizzard. "You might want to get folks to wrap it up and head home while they can still get there," he said.

We paid the bill and trudged out to the parking lot along with everyone else.

I started the Jeep and turned on the heat while George used the snowbrush to sweep off the windows. David might not have been the killer, but he drove a snowmobile and was out of the building for a while. I wasn't ready to cross him off my list of suspects just yet. At least I'd talk to Marc about him first.

CHAPTER ELEVEN

AS DAVID HAD WARNED, the blizzard's force had steadily increased while we were at the Cafe and now at least four inches of fresh snow covered the streets. Neither of us had driven on snow in years and no, it's not like riding a bike.

Marc Clayton lived in an historic Victorian mansion on Foxglove Street, not far from Eagle Creek. The mansion's guesthouse would be our home for the week.

George took it slow and easy and eventually, we reached our destination. Marc had said he'd be back later but had left the cottage door unlocked for us. We unpacked and tromped our way inside.

I wandered around the charming cottage,

examining everything, which didn't take long. Two minutes to tour the entire place.

A cheerful blaze burned in the fieldstone fireplace and freshly baked cookies scented the air. A single bedroom, small kitchen, one bath and an all-purpose room for everything else. The refrigerator had been stocked with my favorite Cuban coffee and the bar contained Glenfiddich scotch for George and Bombay Sapphire gin for me. Marc, an excellent host, had once again thought of everything.

George had walked into the bedroom and plopped down on the bed. "Willa, this is supposed to be a vacation. I need a nap." He wiggled his eyebrows at me, but I was most definitely not in the mood.

For the next week, George and I would have more time together than we'd spent in years. When we'd planned the trip, we'd expected a romantic getaway, but romance and murder rarely mix. So much for plans.

I laid down next to George on the bed and snuggled up for warmth, though. In a few minutes, he was snoring.

When I closed my eyes, I could still see Leo Richards' body slumped over the steering wheel of his Toyota, with a gaping hole in his head through which his life had blasted out.

I imagined the young widow and the young fatherless daughter in mourning.

They'd know by now. Someone would have delivered the horrible message that daddy would not be coming home. Their vague images solidified into vivid pictures behind my heavy eyelids. The stuff nightmares are made of.

George slept and eventually I must have dozed off until a solid, continuous pounding on the cottage door pulled me back to the land of the living.

My eyes popped open and I gave my head a quick, negative shake. I moved a little bit closer to George, but the space next to me was empty and the sheets were cold.

Several more knocks suggested that whoever was at the door wasn't about to leave and George wasn't answering the summons for some reason.

I pushed myself out of bed, slipped my feet into shoes, pulled my sweater tighter around my body and noted George's absence from the tiny abode as I made my way to the front door.

"Where the hell did he go?" I said to the empty room. I took a quick look around, but I didn't see a note.

I pulled back the curtain and peeked out to see the blizzard was now causing a near white-out.

A Michigan State Trooper stood on the porch poised to knock again. I yanked the door open and a strong gust pelted my body with icy snow.

CHAPTER TWELVE

"MA'AM," TROOPER KEMP SAID. He was covered in snow, holding two tall hot cups in black gloved hands. He tipped his head in a gesture of respect and raised one of the cups in my direction. "May I come in? I brought the best coffee in town. I heard you were a caffeine addict."

"Heard from whom?" I asked as I stepped out of the way.

When Kemp was inside and we were snugged up against the elements again, I opened my coffee and he opened the second cup for himself. The double whiff made me swoon. Someone in this town knew how to brew, thank God.

"You must be feeling a little like Typhoid Mary right at the moment," he said after a suitable time for savoring. I looked at him blankly. "You show up here for the first time in ten years and somebody ends up dead."

I said nothing.

His tone was light, teasing. "Does this happen everywhere you go? Or just in Pleasant Harbor?"

My gaze narrowed. So he'd been investigating me. Which is what I should have been doing to him and the victim instead of sleeping. While it was true that I'd had more brushes with murder than most judges, I was in no mood for his humor. I wanted some answers and I wanted them now.

"You've figured out who I am, I take it?"

"Yes ma'am, I have, United States District Judge Wilhelmina Carson. And I also know you have no jurisdiction here." He simply stated the facts. His tone had not turned to belligerence. Yet. But I could feel him going in that direction, which was fine with me. Bring it on.

The jousting restored my equilibrium a bit, although my brain remained fogged with sleep. "All right, then you know that I am not involved in any crimes."

"Never thought you were."

"So tell me what's going on. I think I have a right to know, don't you?"

"Last time we met, I'd have said no, you don't have a right to know. You're a citizen here, like everybody else. You're not even a witness. Nothing but a bystander who found a body. So I'd have said you were entitled to exactly nothing."

Hard to argue with the facts. "I hear a 'but' coming."

"But that was before I talked to Judge Trevor." He flashed a canary-eating grin.

The caffeine hadn't kicked in yet so it took me half a beat longer than it should have to make the connection.

Randy Trevor.

I'd forgotten he was a judge here now. He was a couple of years senior to me at the firm in Detroit where we'd spent our attack-puppy lawyer years. We'd worked on cases together at the bottom of the totem pole before he and his wife, Madeline, decided to move north to Pleasant Harbor to be near both families. He figured he'd get a faster boost up the career ladder here in his home town and he'd been right. He was appointed to the bench long before I was. From time to time we'd chatted at legal events, but otherwise we hadn't spoken to each other in years.

And it must have been Madeline Trevor who

was at the bridge club this afternoon. The woman who'd given me the strange look. The president who so intimidated the hostess. Probably her sisters at the table with her, too.

Kemp nodded when he sensed I'd figured things out. Then he continued, "Judge Trevor wants to see you. He asked me to escort you to his chambers."

While it was true that I had no jurisdiction here, Randy Trevor couldn't compel me to show up in his fiefdom, either. This was a request. Nothing more. Whether he phrased it like one or not. "Did he say why?"

"No ma'am, he didn't. But I suspect he's looking for some experienced help here. We don't have murders like this in Pleasant Harbor. This isn't Detroit. Or even Tampa." Kemp sipped his coffee while he waited for me to agree.

"You've got resources at your disposal, surely."

"We do."

"Why not ask for assistance from one of your colleagues, then?"

Kemp shrugged.

Which was okay. I figured I knew the answer to this one. The situation was similar to a man asking for directions. A very powerful man. A man used to making decisions and telling people what to do. In other words, hell would absolutely freeze over before he'd admit to his colleagues that he needed anything, let alone ask for help on a case if he could get some secret talent off the books.

Which meant I held all the control here. Or at least, control over the next couple of hours.

The way I saw it, I could refuse, which was totally against my nature and wasn't really an option. I'm not one to stand on the sidelines much. Randy Trevor would have remembered that about me. Option two: I could go into a meeting completely ignorant of the situation to joust with a man I didn't really know any more and who did have jurisdiction and probably access to more information than I could get quickly on my own. Better choice: I could wheedle a bit more information from Trooper Kemp before I made up my mind.

The warm coffee I held in my hands seemed to beckon me. I sat at the kitchen table and gestured Kemp toward the other chair as I sipped, stalling, running through things in my head.

I hadn't recovered from the bloody visions behind my closed eyelids during my nap. George had probably walked over to the mansion and he'd be back shortly. He'd be willing to drive in the blizzard, maybe. I loved to drive on the open road with the convertible top down on my car in Tampa. But driving in blizzards and whiteouts? No thanks.

"You know what's going on here, don't you?" I asked. Kemp didn't confirm, but he didn't deny, either. He just drank his coffee and waited. "Don't you think I deserve to be on an equal playing field with everyone else?"

He took his gloves off and got comfortable in the chair, but he kept the big brimmed hat on. I watched him think about things.

After a bit, he said, "Leo Richards, the fellow you found this morning? The murder victim?"

I nodded.

"The situation is a bit more curious than you know. Because he's been missing for more than a year. Almost fourteen months, to be precise."

"What do you mean?"

"He'd been having financial trouble on top of some other family problems and you know how that puts stress on a marriage. January was a year ago, he and his wife had a major blowout. Broken furniture, holes punched in the wall, the whole nine yards. Her sisters were there and all three of them were terrified. He left the house in anger, jumped into that Toyota SUV you almost slammed, and—" he shrugged again.

"He didn't even try to contact his child in all that time?"

"Wife says not."

"What about his job?"

"He had a partner in his hardware business who hasn't seen him in the past fourteen months, either. David Mason. I believe you met him earlier today at Eagle Creek Cafe, didn't you?" Kemp continued to drink his coffee but he watched me closely. How did he know where we ate lunch or that we met Mason?

Somehow, his research on me had included where we went after we left him at the murder scene. That was the important piece of Intel.

"Where did Richards go when he left town?"

"We don't know. Las Vegas, Atlantic City, Detroit. Wherever he could find a casino or a poker table, would be my guess," Kemp said.

"He was addicted to gambling?"

Kemp nodded. "Caused him and his family no end of grief, I can tell you."

Probably created quite a few local enemies, too. Some of them might even be capable of murder.

"Did you try to locate him after he disappeared?"

"He's a grown man. If he wants to desert his family, there's no law against it as far as I know. Not the sort of thing we'd conduct a nation-wide manhunt over, anyway."

"Makes him a deadbeat dad and a sorry human being, though," I said.

"You got that right."

"Didn't the wife try to find him?"

"The family hired a couple of private investigators, I'm told. But they didn't find the guy. People don't want to be found, there are still lots of ways to hide in this country."

"If that's what happened," I said. People are kidnapped for ransom or human trafficking or any number of reasons. But Leo Richards might not fit those victim profiles. I'd need to know a lot more about him than I did now to figure that out.

"Meaning what?"

"There should have been a plane ticket or something," I replied.

"Maybe," he shrugged again. He waited a beat, "Like I told you before, this is a small town. He didn't come home and never went back to work and nobody has seen him since then. He'd ruined a lot of lives already. I'm not sure people cared much about him by then. Guy's gone and good riddance, you know?"

I took a sip of coffee and almost spit it back. Stone cold. I hated reheated coffee, but I needed warm liquid and now was not the time to get all precious about my caffeine. I popped the cup into the microwave for a couple of minutes.

While I waited, I shook my head to clear it of sleep's last cobwebs and asked, "Did you check the mileage? On the Toyota?"

"Yes."

"Loquacious, aren't you?"

"I try."

I grinned. I didn't want to like the guy, but it was hard not to. "And? What did you find out?"

Kemp said, "Well, that's a curious thing, too. The Toyota is about ten years old. Like most vehicles around here, it's got a lot of miles on it. Close to two-hundred thousand. His wife says Leo had the vehicle serviced a few days or so before he disappeared. We checked with the mechanic. He said Leo always took good care of the Toyota and the mileage was close to two-hundred thousand last time he serviced it."

The microwave dinged. I pulled out the cup and took a sip of the heated coffee and burned my tongue. "Crap!" I drew a cold glass of water and swished it around in my mouth, which seemed to help my scalded tongue not one whit.

Kemp looked at his watch. "Judge Trevor is expecting us. We can talk about the rest in the car. Are you going dressed like that?"

Which is when I looked down and noticed I was wearing my pajamas under my cardigan. Now how the hell had that happened? George. Obviously. I hoped.

"I'll be right back," I said, as I ducked into the bedroom to slip into my jeans again. It took me only a few seconds to dress in the warmest clothes I owned. I ran a quick toothbrush around my teeth and finger-combed my pixie-cut. I looked again for a note from George, but found none. In three minutes, I was ready. George says I'm fast, for a girl.

I snagged my parka, gloves, and my miniscule purse and dropped my phone into my pocket, wishing I'd remembered to stick it on the charger before my nap. When I returned to the front door to don the hideously huge boots, Kemp was waiting.

"Do you have any theories about who shot Richards?" I asked him with my hand on the knob and before we opened the door to the blasting snow once more.

"Prevailing theory is the guy the media has been calling the snow sniper."

I halted at the threshold with the door open and the howling wind rushing through, snow swirling around my body. "The what?"

"Let's go. I'll tell you about him in the car." Kemp gave me a little push on the shoulder which made me plant my feet inside the cottage.

"I'm driving my own car," I said.

He laughed and pressed my shoulder forward again knocking me slightly over the threshold where I planted my feet more firmly. He pulled on his gloves. "That'll be some trick. Even if you could navigate in this blizzard. Which I doubt."

I didn't budge. "I've got four-wheel drive and I've driven in blizzards before, Kemp."

He sobered quickly at my steely tone and fierce stare and unrelenting stubbornness. "Yes, ma'am. I'm sure you do and you have. But not today. Because your vehicle's already gone."

I whipped my head around to peer through the white stuff. Sure enough, the driven snow covered everything. Trees, shrubs, trash cans. Everything that is except the missing Jeep.

George Carson. Where the hell did you go?

Kemp gave me a little shoulder nudge again and this time, I stepped out into the storm. He followed me and pulled the cottage door closed. Then he moved around in front of me and led the way to his cruiser, which was now as snow-covered as everything else.

Kemp opened the passenger door and I slipped inside. He closed me snuggly within the cold cruiser and trudged around the front and slipped in behind the wheel. Now that he'd secured me inside the car, he honored his promise to tell me more without prompting. "I'm not sure how Leo Richards was involved with the snow sniper. Maybe there was no relationship between the two at all. As far as we can tell, the sniper killed the other three victims randomly. One thing I just found out a few minutes ago, though."

He fired up the ignition and waited for a bit of warmth before he flipped on the wipers. They struggled to move the heavy snow aside. Maybe he didn't have a snowbrush. "We got the quick and dirty preliminary ballistics report back on the bullet used to kill Leo Richards."

Those quick reports could be wrong. But they could rule out possibilities and narrow the search for the murder weapon. I reached to fasten my seat belt. I was colder than I'd been in years and when I managed to get warm again, I vowed to stay as far away from snow as humanly possible for the rest of my life. Of course, I'd vowed that before and here I was. "What did the ballistics establish?"

"The gun that killed Leo Richards was not the gun used on any of the snow sniper's other victims," he said, reaching his arm out the window and catching the wiper to knock the snow off.

"Did you tell Judge Trevor about that report?"

"Yes, ma'am. Just before I knocked on your door. Doesn't mean the guy owns only one gun, though, you know?" he replied, half a second before he flipped the fan up to full blast on the defroster. After that, all conversation was lost in the wind.

CHAPTER THIRTEEN

BY THE TIME WE headed out of the cottage driveway, we could almost see through the tiny clear space on the bottom of the windshield.

Kemp concentrated on his driving and I thought about what to ask first when we could turn the blasting fan down low enough to hear each other. I wanted to know about the snow sniper and why he was a suspect when the ballistics were wrong on the murder weapon and whether Kemp had any leads and when the sniper would be arrested and a zillion other questions.

But I didn't want him to lose concentration while driving on the snow and black ice my experience said was probably underneath it. So I held my tongue and looked at the slowly passing landscape while I made my mental interrogation list.

The world outside the vehicle resembled a snow globe, everything shaken upside down and filled with the blizzard. The town was picturesque and remote and the pristine white snow covered everything ugly underneath.

What rot lay under the beautiful blanket of false serenity falling softly all around me, making travel difficult and clarity impossible? This was a place where a man could disappear for an entire year and no one mourned or seemed to care. Pleasant Harbor was not so idyllic after all.

Snow continued to fall steadily and Kemp had trouble keeping us between the ditches even in the four-wheel drive vehicle and even without my distracting questions. So my inquisition was delayed.

I pulled out my cell phone, which hadn't rung since we arrived here. Not even once. Today was Tuesday and my courtroom should have been in full swing in the Florida sunshine. My assistant, Augustus, had promised not to call me with trivial questions, but I hadn't believed him. He'd never honored that promise before. There was no reason to think he'd start doing so now.

I pulled off one of the clumsy gloves to glance at the phone's screen. One missed call. Okay. At least I wasn't completely out of touch. The call was from George's cell. He'd left a voicemail. I pushed the button and held the phone to my ear.

The signal had been weak and the message was garbled and cut off too soon. I listened to it three times before I was able to make out a few words that sounded maybe like "…Sorry I didn't leave a note…. Couldn't sleep…. Back soon."

Otherwise, nothing.

I pushed the redial and got a lot of empty air. I tried the internet browser to look up media coverage of the snow sniper, but couldn't connect to that, either. No signals. Which wasn't surprising I guess, given the abominable weather.

I dropped the phone back into my pocket and returned my gaze to peering outside at the blinding white trail ahead of Kemp's squad car.

"What the hell is going on here?" I didn't realize I'd asked aloud until he replied.

"Classic misdirection, I'd say. Wouldn't you?" He held the wheel in a tight grip at the nine and three positions. His body leaned forward as if getting closer to the windshield would improve visibility outside. The cruiser's headlights seemed to make matters worse because they simply illuminated the heavy snow, but Kemp might have thought they made the cruiser more obvious to others and we needed them to avoid a collision or something.

Before I had a chance to ask another question, he raised his voice to say, "The snow sniper is a rather fanciful moniker, but the media types do like to give these killers a handle. The short of it is that we've had three murders in Mid-Michigan before this one, all three had similar characteristics and all were committed by the same weapon. This one is either a change in the killer's method and weapon or it's a copycat."

"Copycat seems the most logical since the ballistics don't match, doesn't it?" I was almost shouting to be heard over the blasting fan and the struggling windshield wipers.

"Probably. There are other differences, too."

"Such as?"

"One thing is the snow sniper has targeted victims from a longer range using a rifle. This one seemed like a rifle shot, but it wasn't. This murder was very up close and personal. And this is the first victim we've found dead in a vehicle. The others were exposed to the shot. One snowmobiler, a cross-country skier, and a woman at a car wash. Fewer logistical issues when the victim isn't surrounded by a steel enclosure."

"I take it these details were withheld from the media? Otherwise, how would a copycat think he could make so many changes and get away with them?"

"I'm a cop, not a mind reader." Kemp might have shrugged, but inside the heavy jacket it was hard to tell. "The good news is that we identified the snow sniper a couple of days ago, but we were still collecting evidence and hadn't arrested him yet. If he killed Richards, then the bad news is another man is dead and we're all looking damn stupid right now. The somewhat better news is that the Richards murder gave us the probable cause we needed to get tight warrants. There's a team on the way to pick him up in Grand Rapids now. So we should know soon enough whether he also owns the Leo Richards murder weapon."

"But you think the snow sniper didn't kill Richards. Aside from wishful thinking, got any evidence?"

Kemp said nothing. Neither did I. He'd answer my question or I wouldn't say another word.

The silence lasted until we finally reached the

Pleasant County Courthouse. We'd traveled the three-mile distance in about half an hour, according to the digital clock in the dash. Not bad, considering the road conditions.

When Kemp pulled into the parking lot, I was relieved to see a county snow plow. Kemp slid into a plowed parking space and turned off the ignition, creating an abrupt and unnerving quiet inside the cabin.

Silently, I pried my hands apart, flexed my shoulders and stretched my neck from side to side, trying to return some blood flow to my severely cramped muscles.

After a moment, Kemp said, "Ready to go?"

I said nothing and didn't move.

He tried to nudge me along. "We're already late. Judge Trevor will explain everything to you when we get inside."

"Tell me why you don't think the snow sniper killed Leo Richards or I'm not going in there. You know the answer. He knows, too. And I don't. We level that playing field right now."

"Actually, you know everything Judge Trevor knows. You're already on that level playing field. Let's go."

I didn't move.

Kemp pulled off his glove and wiped his face with his hand while he thought things through. His research on me must have given him a few examples of exactly how stubborn I can be because as the silence lingered, he took me at my word.

"The murder weapon was a Desert Eagle 50 caliber handgun. Reported stolen last year. It's a match. No doubt about it. That's the weapon that killed Leo Richards this morning."

There was more. I could feel it. "A match to what? And what's the rest of the story?"

He didn't say. I didn't budge.

Kemp sighed. Weary, maybe. Resigned at least. "The weapon was registered to David Mason."

"That's your big secret? David Mason, the chef at Eagle Creek Cafe? His stolen gun was the murder weapon?"

"That's the one. Now let's go." Before I could ask any more questions, Kemp left the cruiser, closing me alone inside. I saw him pulling his gloves over his hands.

After snugging up my gloves, I opened the door and stepped into the blizzard again. Why the hell had I ever thought this frozen white stuff was the least bit romantic?

My boots landed onto a layer of new snow over

the hard pack. The wind nearly knocked me over. My hair became covered with snowflakes in just a brief moment and the icy flakes pelted my face. I flipped up the parka's hood and turned my head down in self-defense.

Kemp walked around the back of the vehicle. I could hear his boots crunching on the snow beside me, but I'd have had to turn my entire body to see him with the parka's hood up. He didn't lock the cruiser, probably because he was afraid the locks would freeze. Or maybe he figured if any fool was willing to come out in this storm to steal the damn thing, they could have it.

"The entrance is this way, Judge." He steadied me by a tight grip on my arm and we made our way cautiously around the building. Kemp pulled hard on the handle of the glass door, sweeping a foot of snow off the entranceway as the door's rubber flashing scraped the concrete and it pivoted open.

I rushed inside and he followed.

After we stamped and dusted off, without another word Kemp led the way down a corridor to our left. We passed two large dark wood doors over which the words "Courtroom A" were posted in brass letters.

The next doorway had white opaque glass on

the top half and wood on the bottom half. The kind of doors you see in old movies from the 1940s. Black letters stood out boldly on the white opaque glass. *Judge Randy Trevor, Pleasant County Circuit Judge.*

Kemp rang a small doorbell to the right. A female voice spoke through the intercom above the button.

"Yes?"

"Trooper Justin Kemp to see Judge Trevor."

A buzzer sounded and Kemp ushered me through another door.

CHAPTER FOURTEEN

WE ENTERED INTO A roomy reception area. The woman who had answered the buzzer sat behind an antique wood desk. Although the building and the office furnishings were old-fashioned, her desk held a thoroughly modern telephone system and better computer equipment than I'd had in Tampa's old federal courthouse before I was allowed to move into newer quarters.

Judge Trevor's secretary, though, could have come from central casting for the same 1940s movie that furnished the office. She looked as if she had been sitting at this very desk since the building was constructed. She was probably sixty years old, but she looked ninety.

She had blue-gray hair, worn in a style that

required a once weekly visit to the salon for a shampoo and set. Glasses so old-fashioned they were trendy framed her eyes, giving her the look of a startled cat. Her white cardigan was held around her shoulders by a sweater clip of plastic pearls. She wore a floral perfume that was vaguely familiar but I couldn't name because my sense of smell was now frozen.

The entire effect was surreal, as if I'd stepped back in time when I crossed that last threshold. I almost expected an old film star to come out of the door to the Judge's chambers any second.

"Hello, Sue," Kemp said in a sweeter tone than I'd heard him utilize until now. "This is Judge Wilhelmina Carson, from Florida. She's staying over at Marc Clayton's guest cottage. We need to see Judge Trevor." Why it was necessary to share all of this information with Sue was beyond me, but I was the guest here.

Sue Evans didn't greet me cheerfully or kindly or in any other way. I might have been invisible for all of the attention she paid to me.

"He's on the phone. Have a seat," she said, barely taking her gaze from the computer screen. I stood near enough to her desk to see she was reading newspaper accounts of the snow sniper's kills. I read over her shoulder, glad that she had enlarged the print about two-hundred percent.

The headline was "Snow Sniper Kills Third Victim at Bayside Carwash." The photographs were winter scenes. Both were exterior views of a do-it-yourself wash stall. A silver mini-van was parked just outside the stall, doors and hatch open, near the coin-operated vacuum cleaner. The vacuum hose rested inside the mini-van's open back hatch. Something dark had stained the carpet, probably blood.

The victim's picture was a grainy formal portrait probably made by an old camera using film. I couldn't read the screen as well as I needed to, but I made out that the victim was shot by a rifle and died instantly. Her identity was withheld pending notification to the family.

One shell casing had been located, but police weren't sure whether the casing was relevant at the time.

Two other shootings were rapidly summarized at the end. One victim was a man sitting on a snowmobile in a parking lot of a convenience store. The other was a woman who had been cross-country skiing. Her body hadn't been discovered for several hours because of her remote location.

Sue must have felt me leaning behind her because she turned and glared at me before she picked up the phone receiver and said, "Trooper Kemp and Judge Carson are here to see you."

A booming, disembodied male voice I recognized even after all these years responded, "Send them in."

Sue inclined her head toward a wooden door on the other side of a latched wood gate. A long buzzer sounded as Trooper Kemp took my elbow again and guided me through. I was beginning to feel like I'd fallen into another world, somehow. A place too quiet, too old, with too many secrets.

When we entered his chambers, Judge Randy Trevor was moving from behind his desk, making his way toward us.

"Willa! It's so good to see you!" Instead of offering to shake hands, he leaned in for a big hug and a tight squeeze that I could barely feel through the parka. He greeted me as if I was a long-lost best friend, when we had only been co-workers a long time ago. I'd never received a warmer greeting from a colleague, including him, even back when we actually knew each other. All of which made me feel suspicious instead of welcomed. What was going on here?

The amenities dispensed with, seated behind his desk with Kemp and me across from him, Judge Trevor got right to the point. "Thanks for coming, Willa. When I saw Justin this afternoon, and he told me you were here, I asked him to see you."

"So he said," I replied.

Kemp had removed his big brimmed hat. Close-cropped red hair and pink scalp, a small nose, freckles across the bridge, a good smile and a pleasant demeanor emerged from the brim's shadow. He seemed wholesome. Under better circumstances, I thought I'd like Justin Kemp quite a lot.

Randy Trevor sat with both elbows on the arms of his chair, his hands clasped together, looking down as if he were praying. Maybe he was. If my jurisdiction was beset by such a killer, I would've been.

"What do you make of all of this Willa?" he asked. "You were always good at figuring things out. Justin tells me you discovered the body this morning. What did you see that we might have missed? What's going on here in my sleepy little town?"

Everyone in Pleasant Harbor knew everyone else. Odds were that the killer was not a stranger to anyone, either. Which meant that Trevor could be involved in all of this somehow. Kemp and Sue Evans, too. My experience and my gut said so, even if the evidence didn't. Yet.

Trevor's professional involvement was fine, albeit premature. No one had been arrested yet and until a suspect was in custody, his role was not official.

Maybe he was curious. Dedicated, perhaps. After all, I had no official role here, either. And yet here I sat. Because Trevor made it so. No one in Tampa would have had that kind of power over me or anyone on our police force. Yet Trevor and others believed he had that power here. Good to know.

I shrugged. "I'm a visitor, Randy. All I know is that you have some pretty bizarre stuff going on in this 'sleepy little town.'" I mimicked his inflection on the last three words. He probably thought I was being snide. I probably was.

Trevor considered something for a few seconds and seemed to make a decision of his own. "Would you mind waiting for us outside, Justin?" Kemp nodded, doing Trevor's bidding once again. How far could Kemp be trusted? I heard the door close behind me.

Judge Trevor leaned forward, placing both forearms on his desk, and refolded his hands into the prayer position. He looked at me with the earnest expression I could remember so clearly it felt like a flashback to an earlier time. A time before snow snipers and murder victims and blizzards and my missing husband. A time when I had nothing to fear from Randy Trevor and he had nothing to fear from me. A lifetime ago.

"Pleasant Harbor *was* a sleepy little town when I moved here ten years ago," he said, ignoring my snide remark. "We've grown a lot since then. Our population, year-round, is low five digits but that's misleading. We get tourists now, winter and summer, sufficient to swell the number of folks to at least ten thousand every weekend."

He raised his water glass and took a sip, then settled more comfortably in his chair. I thought he might actually put his feet on the desk like he regularly did when we were associates, but he didn't.

"What's your point?" I said.

He glared a bit. I was getting under his skin. Good. He might make a mistake I could exploit if he wasn't too comfortable. "Now we have all the problems any other big city has. I get the *New York*

Times delivered to my house every day. My wife wears couture clothes and carries expensive handbags when we go to dinner. And we've got so much crime these days that we're building a big new jail and courthouse complex to deal with it all."

I shrugged. Whatever he thought would impress me in that speech had missed the mark. "My jurisdiction covers several big cities, Randy. But even in Tampa we don't let snipers get away with murder and go on their merry way until the next unlucky motorist happens past."

This time my tone had been more than snide. I was insulting and I didn't really care. He'd hijacked me, not the other way around. He owed me answers, at the very least. I owed him nothing.

Trevor jerked his head back sharply. He was a big man about town here, probably not used to disrespect of any kind. But to me he was just another guy with a government job. Meaning he worked for us, not the other way around. And he was not half as important as he seemed to think. Not to me, anyway.

I rose from my chair. "I've got things to do."

He waved me back. "Okay. Okay."

I gave him my best get-to-the-point stare. The one that works on recalcitrant defendants in my courtroom a lot better than his methods were working on me.

I sat on the edge of the seat this time, letting him see I wasn't making myself too comfortable, the better to get up and go if he didn't stop jerking me around.

CHAPTER FIFTEEN

HE SWIPED HIS HAIR with his open left-hand and a weary sigh escaped his mouth. "It's been hard for David Mason these last few years. He was just getting on his feet again."

So Kemp had lied to me. Trevor did know about the ballistics report after all. He knew David Mason's stolen gun was used to murder Leo Richards. He thought David had done the deed.

"David's family was just coming out of a really bad patch after his business partner gambled away all their assets and disappeared."

Yeah, yeah, yeah. I was a little too tired of the excuses. "And then what?" I prodded.

Trevor sighed again. He stood and began to pace the room, slowly, as if he was creating his story as he went. "I'm not sure exactly. I know that people didn't trust him. He'd had trouble paying his employees. David went to work over at the cafe, which pays enough to keep the wolf from the door, I guess."

"What does any of this have to do with Leo Richards' murder? Or with me, for that matter?"

Trevor bowed his head again briefly before he looked up to give me a steady gaze. "Leo Richards was David's business partner. He's the one who destroyed David and his family. And then he just vanished months ago and left David to handle the mess."

"And David couldn't handle it," I said. "So you're saying David Mason had a good reason to kill Richards, then. Your case is solved. You should be telling Kemp this story instead of me."

Trevor stopped and stared at me with a stunned expression I took to be surprise. "You don't know?" Then, he caught himself and resumed a weary tone. "Not that it matters. Everyone knows."

I waited. He'd spit it out or he wouldn't. I didn't care one way or the other and I didn't see why he'd think I might care.

"David Mason is my brother-in-law. His wife and my wife are sisters," Trevor said.

The weary countenance didn't impress me. I was weary, too. George was missing and I couldn't make it back to the cottage alone. I felt trapped physically, emotionally and intellectually and I struggled against the restraints.

"When did you find out David was coming unraveled?"

Trevor removed his hand from his pocket and wiped his face. "Three weeks ago. David became more and more frantic. Three weeks wouldn't have been a problem, if this was the first time he'd been unable to pay his bills. People are neighborly here. Creditors would have let him slide."

But of course, it wasn't the first time. Far from it, I'd bet.

"People who had been burned before were unwilling to give him a chance. What could he do?" He actually looked at me with innocence in his eyes, as if his excuses for his brother-in-law's criminal behavior were remotely acceptable.

Now it was my turn to be incredulous. And pissed off. "Besides kill Leo Richards you mean?" I stood up and turned to stalk out.

In a flash he was behind me. He grabbed my arm. "Wait," he pleaded. "Please."

I looked at him. "For what?" He still held my

arm. I looked down pointedly at the hand he'd placed to restrain me.

He did not let go. "There is a snow sniper, Willa. The State Police will arrest him today. He killed three people already. He could have killed Leo Richards, too. The snow sniper is a more likely suspect than David. He's killed three times before. *Three times.* He'll be convicted. It won't take long. He could have killed a fourth time. Maybe he did. I need your help, Willa. Will you help me?"

No, I wanted to scream, *I will not help you. And if you don't do your job, I'll make sure you pay for Richards' murder, too. Remember Richard Nixon. It's not the crime, it's the cover up.*

But I didn't say that.

And because I said nothing, he continued, "David Mason is not a bad man, Willa, but he is a desperate one. I know you see desperate people in your courtroom all the time, because I do. Desperate people do desperate things." Still he held my arm, restraining my freedom, making me angrier by the millisecond. "David has a wife. Small children. His family needs him."

As if that made David's actions somehow less heinous, less destructive.

"Leo Richards had a wife and a daughter, too.

You took an oath to uphold the law just like I did, Randy," I told him, shaking my arm so that he'd let me go. "Are you going to do that? Or do I have to do it for you?"

If George and I hadn't stumbled upon the crime scene, David might have escaped detection completely. By the time Kemp arrived at the Toyota this morning, most of the exterior forensic evidence had already been destroyed. Perhaps it would all have been gone, even the ballistics. Randy Trevor would have had his way.

The mere idea heated up my anger like one of those steam tunnels under the old asylum. I was near ready to blow.

What Randy and David had planned seemed like the perfect crime. Randy knew the snow sniper had been identified and would be arrested with just a little bit more evidence. He might have told David about it or maybe David just got lucky with the timing. Either way, David killed Leo thinking the snow sniper would be blamed. His insurance against prison was his brother in law, the one and only judge.

In a town like Pleasant Harbor, Judge Randy Trevor would have enough clout to make something like this go away for David, if David was arrested at all. Trevor shouldn't preside over a case involving his brother-in-law, but who would object? If no one challenged him, there were any number of ways he could have helped David avoid conviction. But if all those methods failed, Trevor could simply give David Mason a suspended sentence, too.

Was my old colleague that corrupt? Would he do that? I could see in his eyes that he would.

"Forget it, Randy. I was there. I saw Leo Richards' brains blown all to hell. David brought the gun and set up the crime. Maybe he didn't mean to kill Leo, but he intended to threaten him, at the very least." I gathered my coat and pulled my gloves out of the deep pocket. "If you think I'm going to let David get away with murder, you have another think coming," I told him as I turned, once again, toward the door.

Trevor put both hands into his pockets and walked around me. He opened the door so that I could walk out. Loud enough for Sue and Kemp to hear, he said "Thank you for coming, Judge Carson." In slightly sinister tones, or at least that's how it sounded to me, he said, "I won't forget this."

I raised my voice slightly to be sure everyone within earshot could hear. "Neither will I. I've been home-towned by better men than you, Randy.

Check it out if you doubt my word. Don't get in my way."

We glared at each other half a moment more before I stalked out.

Kemp followed close behind me as I strode through Judge Trevor's outer office and began the trek across the parking lot. Outside, snow continued to fall in heavy, wet flakes. At least another inch of the white barricade had accumulated since he'd parked the cruiser. Could I walk three miles back to the cottage without freezing to death? Maybe not. But I would damn sure try.

I kicked at the snow and watched it pile up on my boots. The snow was my enemy now, keeping me captive here in this silently hostile world, away from George, away from my beloved Florida sunshine.

Neither Kemp nor I said anything more until we reached the cruiser. As I marched past the door, he laid a restraining hand on my shoulder and I shook it off.

"Don't be so stubborn for once. You'll freeze out here and you won't find a ride in this weather. I can take you back to your cottage, but you know you'll be stuck there until this weather clears. You can't drive anywhere." I kept moving, even as I knew he was right. He grabbed my arm and spun me around to face him. "You'll never get there. Let me drive you. I brought you here. I feel responsible for you."

I said nothing. Was Kemp under Judge Trevor's control now? I'd be a fool to assume otherwise.

"I've lived here all my life, Willa. I know these roads. The county tries, but the plows can't keep up with this much snowfall." He released my arm and opened the passenger door.

CHAPTER SIXTEEN

I WANTED TO KEEP walking, to ignore him, to make it back under my own steam. But I knew he was right. I was more likely to die trying. So I said nothing and struggled into the front seat. He closed me inside and walked around the back of the cruiser.

He settled into the driver's seat, put the key into the ignition and turned it. The cruiser roared to life. He flipped on the windshield wipers, throwing heavy snow onto the ground. Next, he turned up the fan, full blast, and we watched as the cold air fogged the windshield from the inside.

It was the last straw.

The events of the day finally broke through my forced composure.

"Shit!" I said, slamming my hand down on the dash. "How can anybody live in this godforsaken place?"

To my astonishment, Kemp threw back his head and roared with laughter. I stared at him as if he had declared himself a lunatic.

"What's so damn funny?"

He collected himself, but his eyes teared with the effort of contained laughter. "I'm sorry. It's just that—"

"What?" I snapped at him. I grabbed for the door handle to stalk out, or as close to stalking as possible in thigh deep snow, but he didn't move.

"Well, look around you," he gestured a wide arc with his arm. "It's beautiful here. The snow makes everything look like a storybook village."

"Not to me, it doesn't," I told him in a stern tone that sobered his humor quickly. "I see a place where people get killed in their cars. And their killers get away with it."

I bit back my words and didn't say *and threatened by judges* because I wasn't ready to share that with Kemp or anyone else just yet. I needed to sort out how to handle that for myself first. I'd warned Randy Trevor off. But he was dangerous and I didn't know how far he would go. I wasn't afraid of him, but I wasn't ready to take him on, even though I'd told him otherwise.

I tried again to open the door, but Kemp had pushed the door locks and held me captive.

"Look," Kemp said, glancing down at his watch. "It's dark out, already after five o'clock. My shift is over. What if we grab a quick dinner and then I'll make sure you get back and settled in for the night."

I wanted to find George and drive down to Traverse City and catch the first flight out of here. I wanted to sit next to George and hold his hand and talk to him. I wanted to be there when his eyes twinkled and he said, "Hey, what's up, Mighty Mouse?"

But I didn't know where George was or when he would be back. Kemp was right. Again. Dammit. Why had I never listened to George when he wanted me to carry a concealed weapon? Stubbornness actually can go too far. Who knew?

Now that the windows were partially clear, I could see the main road in front of the courthouse was snow blocked again. The plows hadn't been by here in at least an hour, and more fresh snow had piled on top of the old, and it was still coming down fast. It would be the same everywhere, only most roads would be even worse.

The wind was starting to whip up, too. Wind would take some of the humidity out of the air and blow drifts across the roads. Treacherous black ice was impossible to see or tame. If I got stuck out there, I could very well freeze to death. I'd be of no use to anyone suffering from frostbite, or worse.

Reluctantly, I had to agree with Kemp.

But I didn't have to like it.

"Come on," Kemp cajoled. "You need to eat. We're not far from Eagle Creek Cafe. You won't find better food anywhere."

He was right on all points. I might as well have a good meal. I hadn't eaten much today and we had scant provisions at the cottage. I'd be at least a little safer in a place where there were other people. And maybe my phone would work in a more populated place and I could get connected and back in control of my life.

"Okay, Kemp. You've worn me down."

He grinned. "And you can call me Justin, Willa. It'll make dinner conversation less ridiculous," he said as he put the cruiser in gear and slowly made our way through the white drifts covering the roads.

Our progress toward Eagle Creek was glacial. He'd popped the cruiser into four-wheel drive, which helped some with traction, but required an even slower pace. We spent half an hour driving and sliding the two miles to the restaurant.

"His wife, Madeline, is the real power behind the throne. She's got a temper, too. Trevor is an all-around good guy, Willa. He takes care of his family is all. Can't blame a guy for that," Kemp said, eyes staring straight ahead, white knuckled grip on the steering wheel.

"So I figured out," I replied, sarcasm loaded in my tone. I was still mad. Not ready to let my grievances go.

"The family's had a run of bad luck for the past few years," he said.

"*Bad luck?* Is that what you call it around here? Where I'm from, we call that murder and it gets you the death penalty." My hand had a tight grip on the armrest and my feet pressed into the floor helping to keep my balance as Kemp's cruiser struggled and slid and slewed along the snow covered streets.

Kemp glanced briefly toward me, looking for agreement or friendship or something I wasn't prepared to offer. "We don't know that David killed Leo yet. And even if we find out that David did pull the trigger, can you imagine how hard that's got to be on Trevor?"

"Not as hard as it was on Leo Richards, I'll bet," I replied.

"There's six kids involved, you know."

"Six? I'm confused. I thought Leo had two and David had two."

"That's right, but Trevor has two kids also."

"What do the judge's kids have to do with anything? He's sentenced murderers before, surely. His kids have got to know that's his job, even if their friends are involved. Why would they be worried about that?"

"So you'd have Randy Trevor, what, send his brother-in-law to prison and then raise those kids in addition to Leo's and his own?"

"What are you talking about?"

Kemp snorted a little and the corners of his mouth lifted as he nodded his head. "So he didn't tell you, then."

"Didn't tell me what?"

"Trevor didn't tell you that he's related to both David Mason and Leo Richards?"

"He did not. He said Mason and Richards were business partners. He said Mason was his brother-in-law."

"That's all true, as far as it goes. They were business partners, and David is his brother-in-law. But that's not the half of it. Randy Trevor, David Mason and Leo Richards are married to three sisters. This is a tragedy for the entire family, not just a part of the family. They've already lost one husband and father in Leo Richards. You want to send another husband and father to prison in David Mason. And then what? Judge Trevor takes on the whole family?"

So that was Randy Trevor's dilemma. He wanted to protect his wife's family. Judges aren't gods. We have lives. We have families. We have feelings. So his desire was understandable.

But he was a judge. He had responsibilities that came with the job. If he couldn't, or wouldn't fulfill his oath to administer blind justice in this case, the very least he should do was to recuse himself and let an impartial judge take over.

He was using his power for his own self-interest. Which meant he was corrupt. He'd lose his job and be disbarred. Three families would be ruined for sure if Randy Trevor continued down this path.

I said, "The wives aren't helpless, you know. Those six kids have mothers, too."

"You met them all today. At the bridge club. In birth order, Madeline, Maureen, and Molly. The 3Ms, folks call them around here. From an old line Pleasant Harbor family. Did they look like they were capable of taking care of themselves to you?" he replied.

The comment irked me so my words were a bit too testy. "Here's some advice that may save your life, Kemp. Never underestimate a woman. Every cop should know that much."

Kemp grinned and nodded. He'd have tipped his hat again, if he'd been wearing one. "Noted."

I said, "So Leo is married to Maureen, the middle sister from a prominent family. And he's missing for fourteen months. And nobody does anything about that? That doesn't seem reasonable to me. Does it to you?"

Kemp might have shrugged again. He said, "The mileage on the Toyota bothers me more. Even if he only drove down to Traverse City and stashed the vehicle somewhere and flew out and drove back to where we found him, the SUV should have more miles on it."

I thought again about the victim's unusually pink skin. There were only two causes I could think of, and neither one of them made any sense. Too many anomalies in this case, for sure.

We'd finally arrived at Eagle Creek. Kemp's vehicle plowed two fresh ruts through the snow in the parking lot and slammed into a snow pile higher than the cruiser.

CHAPTER SEVENTEEN

MOST PEOPLE HAD ENOUGH sense to stay home on a night like this. But there were two vehicles I recognized parked close to the entrance. A silver Cadillac I'd noticed there earlier today. The other was our rented Jeep. Parked in the same place George had placed it at lunch.

So this is where you are. The knowledge made me feel both better and worse. I was relieved he wasn't dying in a ditch somewhere, of course. But also damned annoyed that he hadn't let me know he was okay. Now that I knew he wasn't dead, I considered killing him myself for scaring me. Figuratively, of course.

I checked my cell phone for messages again. Nothing. The storm must have done something more permanent to the cell network than I'd hoped. I hadn't received a call in the past several hours and I knew both George and Augustus would have tried to reach me.

I dialed George's cell phone, but nothing happened. "Great," I said under my breath to no one. "Just great."

Kemp backed up slightly away from the snow mound, shut down the wipers and the lights, and turned off the ignition. "Just think about it, Willa. You're a fair judge, they tell me. Find out all the facts before you decide what's fair here. Can't you do that much?"

I made no promises. Partly because the identity of the murder weapon wasn't the only thing we knew. At this point, David satisfied the three classic criteria every killer possessed: means, motive, and opportunity. Richards had gambled away David's livelihood and left David saddled with at least half the responsibility for Richards' family, if Kemp's appeal was true. He'd been out on his snowmobile this morning when the crime occurred, which meant he had opportunity to commit the crime.

David might not be the killer, but Kemp should be looking at him pretty damn hard.

After bundling up again, gloves and hood in

place, we exited the cruiser and trekked toward the wide porch overhang in front of Eagle Creek Cafe's door. About half-way across the parking lot, Kemp turned toward the road we'd just left and said, "Look. Look out there and tell me this place isn't beautiful."

I cast my gaze on Eagle Creek Cafe's surroundings. Evergreen trees, blue spruce, and hemlock pines were laden with heavy snow coating their branches like thick frosting. The never-ending snow, now that I'd accepted it as my constant cloying companion, did seem soft and lacy. Indeed, it was a gorgeous setting.

But I preferred open roads and sidewalks, Hillsborough Bay and palm trees. I wanted to go back to Tampa. I was beginning to feel like Dorothy Gale and I wished I possessed a pair of magic ruby slippers.

We started another trek through the heavy snow. As he had before, Kemp walked in front of me to clear a path. I followed a few feet behind, paying attention to the uneven terrain and struggling to keep my balance on the rough stones beneath the snowpack.

After we'd traveled a few yards, I raised my head and turned my body to look around. Across the gray darkness, floodlights dotted the landscape and perversely contributed to my night blindness. Still, I saw something strangely menacing. What was that? A snowmobile? I hadn't heard its engine, but it was less snow covered than George's Jeep or the silver Caddy. What was it doing way over there? Where was its rider? The snowmobile could belong to David Mason. In fact, the more I thought about it, the more likely it seemed.

The flat parking lot was better lit than the surrounding lawns. Outside the light halos, shadows swayed buffeted by the harsh gale. I squinted through the heavy snowfall, which didn't improve my weak distance vision any.

But I definitely saw something.

Two white tail deer? A couple of black bears? Or Mason with someone else?

They were too far from me and moving away and there was too much blinding snow. But they didn't look right. Call it instinct or whatever. I don't know. But it was damned odd.

Kemp had tromped ahead toward the entrance, breaking a trail.

"Justin!" I shouted, but the wind carried my voice in the opposite direction. He plowed onward, head down, focused on reaching his goal.

I looked again at the receding shadows across the distance. The two had separated slightly. Now they looked more like humans wearing parkas with huge hoods, similar to mine. But what the hell were they doing out there in the no-man's land between renovated grounds and hardwoods in this blizzard? Where could they possibly be going?

"Willa!" Kemp's voice came at me weakly as if from a wide distance, pulling my gaze from the shadows. "Willa! Come on!" He stood on the porch at the entrance door to Eagle Creek Cafe, waving me down the path he'd stomped moments before that was already filling with fresh drifts.

I waved back and pointed toward the shadows. By this time, they'd trudged far outside the light halos and deeper into the blinding blizzard. Kemp was fifty feet from where I stood. He probably couldn't see them at all.

As I watched, they moved into another light pool. The one cast by a stronger floodlight above the narrow wooden door that covered the entrance to the steam tunnels underneath the old hospital. The door was padlocked. Only the tour guide and the maintenance supervisor had keys, I'd been told when I took the tour years ago.

One of the shadows raised something heavy and

bashed it down hard on the door. Then, he pushed the door open and he shoved the other shadow into the narrow opening and then followed and the door swung closed.

They were going down into the old steam tunnels. There was nothing down there but damp, cold, blackness. Spiders. Snakes. And dead critters of all sorts. I shuddered.

The tunnels stretched through the entire complex and once provided state-of-the-art steam heat for buildings that stretched out more than half a mile before the hospital was condemned years ago. The two shadows could walk from there through the tunnels into the main building. Maybe the snowmobile broke down. Maybe they simply wanted to get out of the blizzard for the rest of their travel.

But it didn't feel like that to me.

What made more sense is that they were headed in the opposite direction. Toward the new hospital and the parking garages. They could have driven there, too. So for whatever reason, they didn't want to be seen.

"Come on!" Kemp shouted, moving his left arm in a big arc as if he could herd me from the storm and into warm safety.

I mirrored the same gesture Kemp had made, guiding him my way before I turned, pulled off my oversized glove so I could fish out my cell phone and use the flashlight app to reveal the snow in front of me.

I began to trudge, raising each leg as high as I dared and carefully placing each heavy boot flat into the snow mound ahead, with deliberate speed.

Away from Kemp. Toward the tunnels.

CHAPTER EIGHTEEN

AFTER AN EXHAUSTING SLOG, I finally reached the green door. Heavy on its antique hinges, it rested open slightly. A thin ribbon of yellow light rimmed the edge, meaning the emergency bulbs burned inside.

A shiny silver padlock hung open on the rusty hasp. Maybe that meant a planned return through this exit instead of a one-way trip to a building or a different escape route.

Exertion and stress sweat trickled down from my armpits, clammy and cold.

I looked for Kemp behind me. He was taller, heftier and thus able to plow through faster than I had done. Still, he was fifty feet back.

The tunnels were warm and snow free.

"Kemp! I'm going down!" I shouted into the wind. He didn't hear me. I arced the app's flashlight beam a few times and hoped he glanced up to notice. Then I turned off the app and stowed the phone in my pocket. I pushed the green door as wide as I could and left it propped open by the snow bank before I ducked into the narrow stairway that led down into the tunnels.

Dank odors assaulted my nostrils. I pulled off the bulky gloves and stuffed them into my pockets and hurried as quickly as I dared in the huge boots down the narrow stone staircase, hanging onto both clammy side rails, deeper into the earth.

The tunnels were below basement level of the old building. Which meant maybe twenty feet or more below the surface. Emergency bulbs encased in metal baskets cast an eerie glow over the ancient bricks.

When I reached the bottom of the stairs and stepped a foot or two into the tunnel, balancing awkwardly on the sloped and slimy floor, I saw three travel options. Straight ahead east. Left north or right south.

Which way did the shadows go?

I heard my own heavy breathing, but no sounds

from the two who had entered barely five minutes before.

No sound from Kemp behind me yet, either.

The east tunnel was short, maybe less than fifty feet ahead where it dead-ended under the front parlor of the building. There was no exit at that point, I remembered.

The north and south tunnels ran a quarter mile each in opposite directions. Exits once existed every one hundred feet or so, but several had been permanently closed.

The north tunnel led to the residences and a parking garage and, eventually, to the new hospital.

The south tunnel led to the basement of the Eagle Creek Cafe building. I couldn't remember how far away the exits were.

Which way did the two shadows travel? I could have called out to them. But should I have?

Before I could make a decision, someone turned the lights out. Instant total blackness. Which probably meant they'd found an exit and left me inside here. No worries. I'm not claustrophobic.

The green exit door was still unlocked. I could leave, trek outside in the blizzard the way I'd entered. All I needed to do was find the staircase and walk up.

But I couldn't see anything. At all. No ambient light of any kind. A wrong move in any direction could send me tumbling onto the cobblestone or worse. I could feel along the tunnel walls until I reached the opening, but my sense of direction was impaired by sensory deprivation, too. I wondered whether this was how a blind person felt navigating in the world.

I pushed my hand down into my pocket and patted around for my cell phone. When I pulled it out and pressed the home button, the screen lit up brighter than stadium lights. The battery was almost gone, but for now, until I could find the light switch, I could see.

I heard footsteps above and behind me. I turned and pointed my phone toward Kemp who had stopped when the lights went out. He'd been on his way down the stairs, gun drawn.

"There's no need for that, Justin. I'm fine. Whoever I followed in here must have left. Can you just reach back and flip—" the rest of my words were stolen by gunfire.

The first shot was true. It whizzed past my head and hit Justin square on the shoulder with enough force to knock him backward. He lost his footing and fell down the last three steps and banged his head soundly against the stone, which knocked him out cold.

His momentum pushed his body into me and I stumbled backward onto the slimy tunnel floor and dropped my phone. I scrambled over the slippery cobblestones to get to it before the screen light shut off and we were plunged into blackness again.

But Kemp had fallen right into my path.

I fumbled to crab over him, but before I reached across his slender torso, the screen shut off, plunging me into total darkness half a moment before the second gunshot whizzed past. I heard the ricochet and more hits before the noise stopped.

I rolled across Justin's body and slid to the opposite side, patting around the slimy rocks for my phone. When my hand bumped something soft and squishy a quick gasp escaped my mouth.

In the black silence my gasp doubled as a beacon for the third gunshot.

I clamped my lips together, hard, and forced my hands to feel along the disgusting tunnel floor, but patted nothing remotely like my phone.

Shit!

The fourth gunshot rang out and this one didn't bounce off the walls. It hit someone. I heard a man's groan followed by hard scrabbling grunts and groans that sounded like a struggle.

I could see nothing. The effect was surreal.

The fifth shot. An unmistakable human female scream was followed by total silence.

I counted silently, "One thousand one. One thousand two. One thousand three." I made it all the way to one thousand twenty eight before the emergency lights came back on.

I saw my phone had been mere inches from my hand and grabbed it. Kemp's gun was close, so I grabbed that, too. I pushed the power button on my phone and nothing happened. Maybe the battery drained or maybe the phone didn't survive the slam against the tunnel floor. Either way, the result was the same. No light. No nothing. *Dammit!*

Then I looked around wildly, prepared to duck again but there was no wall to hide behind. Kemp groaned, perhaps returning to consciousness. His wound was bleeding profusely, adding to the slime.

I looked north and south, but the tunnel curved in each direction, cutting off my sight line. Was the gunman hiding around the corners? Or had he found an exit and already escaped?

In the east tunnel straight ahead, I saw the

shadow that looked something like an apparition, but knew it had to be a person. Man or woman, I couldn't discern. Nor did it matter. Because it was holding the gun.

So I took a chance. The most logical option.

"Mason! Kemp's been shot!" I shouted, and immediately realized my voice was too loud. I lowered it a couple of notches. "David, I know what happened to Leo Richards." Which wasn't completely true. But I'd figured out enough to make a plausible guess. "He's been dead for months, hasn't he? His murder was staged today to make him look like a victim of the snow sniper. Did you kill him, David?"

I heard his ragged breathing. His deep voice confirmed my guesses. "No. I didn't."

"Who did kill Leo? Who's there with you?"

"I've been shot." He leaned against the tunnel wall and lowered the gun. "Get help, Willa. Before it's too late."

For a moment, I paused. Should I try to leave? He'd recognized me. Could David Mason be trusted not to shoot me when I stood up and became a bigger target?

"David, who is with you? How is she?"

Kemp needed help right away. For the woman,

it might already be too late. She'd been completely silent. She could be unconscious. Or worse.

"Madeline Trevor. Ricochet hit." David's voice was breathless, weak.

"You mean it's Randy Trevor's wife?" I called back to confirm we were talking about the same person, which was a bit inane under the circumstances. I'd seen Madeline Trevor at the bridge club. She'd looked at me oddly, with what I now realized must have been suspicion. Maybe her husband had told her something about me. Or maybe she remembered me from back in the day. Either way, my presence must have pushed her over the edge.

"I don't know how bad," Mason said. "She planned to kill me. Leave me here." He seemed to have only enough wind to speak a few words each time. "I'd told her we'd had enough. She pulled a gun. She wanted to kill you. I tried to stop her. We struggled, but the gun went off. I didn't shoot at you, Willa. I swear." His voice was weaker with each short sentence.

Now that the emergency lights were on, I could see the steps leading to the green door and the blizzard, which all of a sudden seemed way less threatening than it had half an hour before. I checked Kemp's carotid pulse. Still beating. But he remained unconscious. No way could I get him up the steps.

"If I stand up, David, you're not going to shoot me, are you?" Not that I would trust his answer, but I wanted to keep him talking while I figured out what to do.

"Madeline shot at you. I didn't," he replied.

David slid down the tunnel wall and sat on the slimy floor. That decided me. No one would sit on that floor if they had a choice.

"I'm going for help. Don't move." I patted around in Kemp's pockets but didn't find his cell. "I need a phone. Mine's ruined. Do you have one?"

"Madeline does."

"I'm coming to get it. Don't shoot me." I walked gingerly over the slimy cobblestones, holding onto the tunnel wall to keep my balance. The last thing I needed was to fall again.

When I reached Madeline Trevor I checked for her carotid pulse, but found none. I patted her pockets until I found her phone, pulled it out of her pocket and dropped it into mine.

I turned to look at David Mason. He seemed to have passed out.

"I'll be right back. Kemp's a police officer. If he

dies, you'll be in even bigger trouble than you already are. Stay put," I said. Would he do it? I didn't know. But I had to get help for Kemp. I had no choice.

I backed out of the tunnel, keeping a watch on Mason to be sure he didn't raise the gun. When I reached Kemp, I stepped over him, pulled myself up the steps, keeping as low a profile as I could, both hands on the rusty rails, until I burst into the night air. I ducked inside again and called down.

"David, I can see you from here. If you move, I'll turn off the light. You won't be able to get away in the dark." I flipped it off for a couple of seconds to prove I could and then flipped it back on. "Stay put."

No reply.

I reached into my pocket and pulled out Madeline's phone. When I pushed the button, her screen powered on and I almost whooped for joy. Until I saw the text notification that rested there.

I read it twice before the screen turned off. It was a text from her husband, Judge Randy Trevor. Only four words. "Is Mason dead yet?"

EPILOGUE

TWO DAYS LATER, GEORGE and I were once again seated at the back table at Eagle Creek Cafe, waiting for Marc Clayton. We'd taken a quick walk through the tunnels because George wanted to see where Madeline Trevor had died. The exit from the tunnels closest to the restaurant would have put her just inside the Cafe entrance. Her plan had been to leave Mason's body in the abandoned east tunnel and then return to the Cafe to complete her alibi. A plan that would have worked if I hadn't seen them across the parking lot that night.

Marc joined us, bringing hot coffee. "Sorry I'm late. I stopped off at the hospital to check on David Mason and Justin Kemp. They'll both recover. Kemp's shoulder surgery will take a little longer than David's abdominal wounds, though both of them will be able to return to work fairly soon."

"What about Randy Trevor?" George asked. He was still a bit angry about him and his wife. George is very protective of me and he takes a dim view of people trying to shoot me. Which I appreciate, of course.

"He's been transferred to jail in Grand Rapids for now," Marc said. "So, Willa, tell me what happened."

I leaned in and folded my hands around the warm coffee mug and wondered if I'd ever be warm again. "When we saw Leo Richards in his Toyota, his skin was unusually pink. I'd seen that before and heard testimony from medical examiners about it, but I couldn't recall the cause. It's similar to the cherry red hue bodies have when carbon monoxide poisoning is the cause of death. Pink *livor mortis* results when a body has been frozen."

"Ah," Marc said.

"When I remembered that, I knew that Richards was colder than he would have been if he'd simply been sitting after death in the Toyota in winter weather."

"Well, if he was already dead, why'd they shoot him in the head?" George wanted to know.

"To conceal the real cause of death."

"Which was what?" Marc asked.

"According to the statement the police took from Leo's wife, the cause of death was blunt trauma to the right temple. The bullet entered his left temple and destroyed the right side of his head with the exit wound. That obliterated most of the evidence that he'd been hit hard enough to kill him. A good forensic autopsy might still have found the real cause, but they had at least a fifty-fifty chance the coroner would miss it simply because the gunshot wound was substantial and sufficient." I explained the rest of the story as we finished our meal.

The whole thing had been a family affair.

There was a big fight fourteen months ago, as Kemp had originally told me. But what the sisters left out at the time was that during the fight, Madeline had killed Leo Richards. He'd been out of control in an argument with his wife and her sister had bashed his head in when she hit him too hard with a heavy bookend to stop him.

The three sisters hid the body in Maureen's basement chest freezer and concocted the disappearance story to cover up. Then they simply tried to carry on normally.

Until things began to fall apart.

When David discovered the extent of Leo's gambling losses and damage to the hardware business, David hired a private detective to find him. David's wife, the youngest sister Molly, begged him to stop looking for Leo, but David said he'd never, ever do that. That Leo needed to come back and face his responsibilities. So Molly told David about the murder to gain his cooperation.

Madeline was having trouble holding it together, too. Her behavior became so erratic that her husband, the judge, confronted her and she broke down and told him. Randy took control, which didn't surprise me in the least. He held everyone together to cover up the crime until the snow sniper came along and gave them all a chance to end the charade.

Randy knew about the impending arrest of the snow sniper. It was his idea to set up Richards' death as another snow sniper victim and to shoot Richards in the left temple to cause the exit wound to obliterate evidence of the blunt force trauma that had actually killed him. Madeline, Molly, and Maureen pulled off the setup and then attended the bridge club tournament to establish an alibi.

"Leo's wife, Maureen, gave a full confession this morning," I said, wrapping things up.

Marc pursed his lips and shook his head. George nodded. There was nothing more to say, really.

It was the pink skin that should have tipped me off to this elaborate cover up. Leo Richards' body was too pink. I knew that pink came from being frozen and then thawed. But I missed it because the weather was so cold, I thought his body temperature was caused by the atmosphere. Turns out it was caused by his cold family.

George remained angry for a good long while, but his trademark sense of calm returned. We stayed to enjoy Pleasant Harbor for the full week and enjoyed a few of the cozy evenings we'd planned before we returned to Tampa.

I may not have owned a pair of ruby slippers and Madeline Trevor wasn't the Wicked Witch, but the entire episode reminded me that there's no place like home.

THE END

Want to find out how The Hunt for Justice began?

Read on for an excerpt of

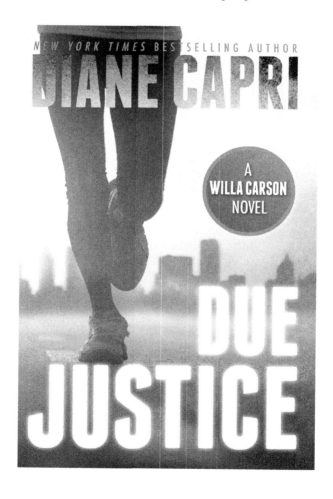

CHAPTER ONE

I GREW UP OUTSIDE Detroit, where the weak were killed and eaten. Still are.

Every morning during my high school years, my clock radio blasted me awake with morning news: *Five men killed last night in Cass Corridor. Two hundred homicides this year.*

Like sports statistics, only bloodier.

Somehow it never occurred to me to change the station.

Even so, murder was far removed from my suburban life. Eventually I moved to Tampa for sunny charm, Southern hospitality, smiling grocery clerks, polite neighbors, small-town feel.

And no crime. Okay, less crime.

But lessons learned young stick with us. All those Detroit homicides proved one thing to me: You never see the bullet that gets you, even when it hits you right between the eyes.

Of course, I didn't think about any of this until long after the time to duck.

Carly Austin ambushed me at home. I'd dashed home from work later than I'd planned. Preoccupied. Distracted. Too much to do, too little time to do it. And there she was. Waiting for me.

Her mere presence was a shock; she'd been ignoring me for more than a year.

I covered well; offered smiles, hugs. Asked her to join me for drinks. She feigned reluctance, but allowed me to persuade.

Twenty minutes later we sat outdoors on the Sunset Bar patio. I played with the pink flamingo swizzle stick in my iced Bombay Sapphire and tonic, moving the lemon twist around the cubes, afraid to sip because the alcohol would do what alcohol does. The swirling gin, yellow lemon and white ice mesmerized, passed the time.

Perfect late January afternoon. Warm and clear.

Setting sun and rising full moon cast simultaneous glow on Hillsborough Bay, giving a mystical quality to my experience.

I knew it was the atmosphere that made me feel this way because I hadn't swallowed any gin. Yet.

Carly's visit was urgent in some way; she never came to me bearing good news or even minor trouble.

I felt my muscles tense with anticipation and anxiety.

Sought understanding. Gaze lifted. Watched my almost-sibling. What was the problem? Sure I could handle it, if only she'd tell me what it was. Too much drama. With Carly, always. If only she'd come tomorrow, when everything in my world was scheduled to be less tense. She had to know that today wasn't the best time to commandeer my attention.

Something was very wrong.

Again I noted the setting sun reflected glistening orange that flattered her copper coloring; but her clothes were wrinkled and dark circles under her eyes showed through her concealer. Lipstick smeared. Bright pink blush on pale cheeks made her look more like Bozo than Garbo. Even her curly red hair was dirty.

So not-Carly.

More gin. Definitely. But not yet.

I felt the familiar ambivalent emotions Carly always inspired. She was fiercely independent, but perpetually getting into some mess that I had to get her out of. I loved her, of course; she was the only sister I'd ever have. But I could strangle her sometimes. Gleefully.

Stubborn as an elephant, she couldn't be pushed. Believe me. I've tried.

While I waited for her to speak I flashed back to the first time we met. Gathered around the bassinet, watching. Instantly beloved. Tiny face, flashing blue eyes. Red ringlets framed porcelain skin. Mom cooed over Carly's little feet and perfect hands. Her brothers murmured in hushed wonder as they examined miniscule fingernails, perfect eyelashes. One of the boys, not quite ten and very clever, wanted to call her Curly, but his mother insisted on Carly, and his brother punched him in the arm whenever he refused to get it right.

No one noticed me, Wilhelmina, standing off to the side, already five foot six and still growing. Nothing about me was petite or cute, then or now. I was gawky and awkward. Even my earlobes were big.

The only things Carly and I had in common were red hair and double X chromosomes.

And her family.

My relationship with Carly was born in that minute. Conflicting feelings of awe, jealousy, irritation—and protectiveness. I've always taken care of Carly and she's always resisted. She thought she could take care of herself. Experience proved otherwise.

I like to think we've both matured in 29 years, but maybe not.

She was all grown up now, but still 110 pounds and 5'2". Carly's style was anything but cute. Sporting brightly polished artificial claws and perfect makeup, she was a proud glamour hound. "It's better to look good than to *be* good" is her personal creed.

Maybe she *can't* be good, or maybe she just doesn't try. Either way, the result is the same: whirling dervish in a small, perfect package.

I sighed loudly. Stopped playing with my watery gin and pushed it aside. As much as drinking would have helped, I'd need to keep all my wits about me to deal with Carly, and I was now dangerously short of time.

Too soon, my husband expected more than six

hundred guests to attend an AIDS research benefit here in his restaurant. It's no secret that I hate these shindigs. Not my thing. At all. George might actually have been holding me captive when he extracted my promise to act as hostess. A thousand dollars a plate. Movers and shakers and poseurs showing up to see and be seen at what they considered their finest. I was hot, sweaty, and still wearing my work clothes.

"Okay, the suspense is killing me. I don't know what it is you have on your mind, but it can't be that bad." Realizing I was sticking my neck out, I asked, "What's up?"

As if she'd been waiting for me to ask, Carly said, "It's worse than anything you can imagine."

She said it quietly, with none of her usual bravado.

Impatience deflated like a bayoneted blimp.

"Hey, come on. I have quite an imagination," I joked. "Just because you haven't talked to me in a while doesn't mean I don't care about you."

The truth was that I cared too much. Always had. Never figured out how to toughen up my heart where Carly was concerned.

She smiled a little, sheepishly; seemed to take the edge off.

Carly slumped back in her chair and looked at the water. There were a couple of late afternoon sunfish sailors out, racing back and forth from Davis Islands to a spot 100 yards off the edge of our island, Plant Key.

About a year or two later, or at least it seemed that long as I imagined myself forced to greet senators and celebrities wearing nothing but my underwear, Carly finally started to talk. I resisted the urge to cheer.

"Did you see NewsChannel 8 this morning?"

"Why?"

More silence.

She picked up her white wine, took a sip, put it down, picked up the blue paper cocktail napkin, concentrating hard while she folded it into a fan. She never looked directly at me.

I wondered if my deodorant would hold on another eight hours. Maybe I could skip my bath?

"Did you see the news story on the drowning victim?" She finally asked, in a small voice.

Drowning victim? Are you kidding me?

Maybe he drowned, but I hoped he was dead before he went into the water.

Frank Bennett had the report. He'd said pieces

of a body were pulled out of Tampa Bay before dawn. The largest portion, the part the sharks hadn't eaten, was found banging against the pilings of the Sunshine Skyway Bridge in Pinellas County. Hands and feet were bound together by clothesline and tied to heavy cement slabs. Face unrecognizable.

By now, she had shredded the cocktail napkin into tiny blue pieces and dropped them all over the deck. I remember thinking foolishly that she'd need collagen on those frown lines next week if she didn't relax.

I nodded encouragement to keep the words flowing because I couldn't fathom Carly involved in murder. The possibility didn't surface.

"Let me ask you a hypothetical question," Carly said.

That very second, I knew. She wasn't looking for sisterly advice. Not the usual boyfriend trouble or help with credit card bills. Carly was involved in something much, much worse. My body shivered with visceral certainty even before my brain acknowledged.

I should have stopped her right there. Should have cloaked us both with appropriate protections. I knew what to do. I knew how to do it.

But did I even try to dodge the bullet I saw coming straight at me? No. So how much smarter had all those Detroit homicides made me?

ABOUT THE AUTHOR

Diane Capri is a *New York Times*, *USA Today*, and worldwide bestselling author.

She's a recovering lawyer and snowbird who divides her time between Florida and Michigan. An active member of Mystery Writers of America, Author's Guild, International Thriller Writers, Alliance of Independent Authors, and Sisters in Crime, she loves to hear from readers and is hard at work on her next novel.

Please connect with her online:

Website: http://www.DianeCapri.com
Twitter: http://twitter.com/@DianeCapri
Facebook: http://www.facebook.com/Diane.Capri1
http://www.facebook.com/DianeCapriBooks

If you would like to be kept up to date with infrequent email including release dates for Diane Capri books, free offers, gifts, and general information for members only, please sign up for our Diane Capri Crowd mailing list. We don't want to leave you out! Sign up here:
http://dianecapri.com/contact/

Printed in Great Britain
by Amazon

19513122R00099